STORY AND ART BY

NORIYUKI KONISHI

ORIGINAL CONCEPT AND SUPERVISED BY LEVEL-5 INC.

YO-KAI WATCH

Volume 3

JIBANYAN'S TALE

Perfect Square Edition

Story and Art by Noriyuki Konishi

Original Concept and Supervised by LEVEL-5 Inc.

Translation/Tetsuichiro Miyaki
English Adaptation/Aubrey Sitterson
Lettering/William F. Schuch
Design/Izumi Evers
Editor/Joel Enos

YO-KAI WATCH Vol. 3
by Noriyuki KONISHI

Printed in the U.S.A.

Published by VIZ Media, LLC
P.O. Box 77010
San Francisco, CA 94107

10 9 8 7 6 5 4 3 2
First printing, January 2016
Second printing, May 2016

STORY AND ART BY
NORIYUKI KONISHI

ORIGINAL CONCEPT AND SUPERVISED BY LEVEL-5 INC.

CHARACTER INTRODUCTION

NATHAN ADAMS

AN ORDINARY ELEMENTARY SCHOOL STUDENT. WHISPER GAVE HIM THE YO-KAI WATCH, AND THEY HAVE SINCE BECOME FRIENDS.

WHISPER

A YO-KAI BUTLER FREED BY NATE, WHISPER HELPS HIM BY USING HIS EXTENSIVE KNOWLEDGE OF OTHER YO-KAI.

JIBANYAN

A CAT WHO BECAME A YO-KAI WHEN HE PASSED AWAY. HE IS FRIENDLY, CAREFREE AND THE FIRST YO-KAI THAT NATE BEFRIENDED.

BARNABY BERNSTEIN

NATE'S CLASSMATE.
NICKNAME: BEAR.
CAN BE MISCHIEVOUS.

EDWARD ARCHER

NATE'S CLASSMATE.
NICKNAME: EDDIE.
HE ALWAYS WEARS HEADPHONES.

KATIE FORESTER

THE MOST POPULAR GIRL IN NATE'S CLASS.

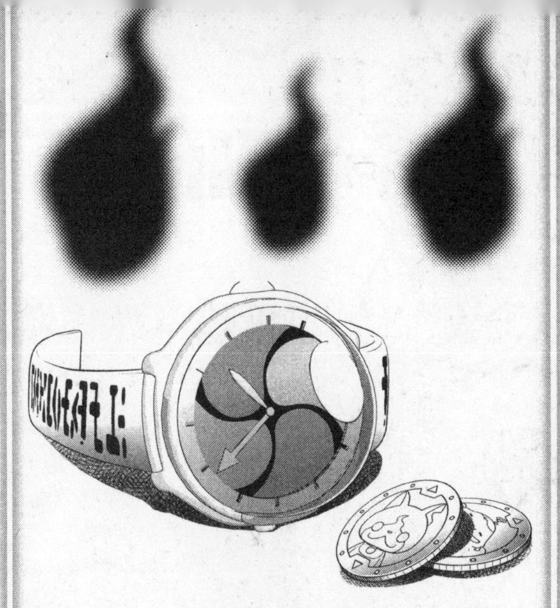

Table of Contents

CHAPTER 15:
YO-KAI SWIMMING
LESSONS!
FEATURING BUTLER YO-KAI WHISPER!

DINGDING DINGDING
TOMORROW WE'LL BE SWIMMING DURING P.E.!
DON'T FOR-GET TO BRING YOUR SWIM-SUITS!
WHAA AAA
I'M NATE ADAMS.
AN ORDINARY ELEMEN-TARY SCHOOL STUDENT.

TWEET TWEET TWEET
WHAT'S WRONG, NATE? YOU SHOULD BE ENJOYING YOURSELF!
TADAA AAAAH
YOU'RE ENJOYING YOURSELF ENOUGH FOR THE BOTH OF US...

HEH HEH HEH, SUMMER IS...
UNNNNNNN
AND THIS IS WHISPER, A YO-KAI.

FOOOOOOSH
...YO-KAI SEA-SON!
HA HA HA HA HA HA HA HA
YOU MEAN GHOST SEA-SON?
G-G-G-GHOSTS ?!
TWITCH...

I DON'T HAVE TIME FOR YOUR JOKES, WHISPER. I'M TOO STRESSED ABOUT TOMOR-ROW.

?

WHA AAAA
GHOSTS AND YO-KAI AREN'T THE SAME THING?!
NO WAY!
SHOULDN'T HE KNOW THAT?!
FOR SOME REASON HE THINKS HE'S MY BUTLER.

HUUUUUH?!
WHAAAA-AAAT?! YOU MEAN YOU CAN'T SWIM?!
KEEP IT DOWN!

MURMUR
MURMUR
MURMUR
OTHER PEOPLE CAN'T SEE YO-KAI.
THEY CAN'T EVEN HEAR THEM.
ACCORDING TO WHISPER, ALL THE STRANGE AND UNPLEASANT THINGS IN THIS WORLD...
...ARE BECAUSE OF HIDDEN YO-KAI!
FWUMP
SPLASH SPLASH
OH! MAYBE I CAN'T SWIM BECAUSE SOME TYPE OF YO-KAI IS HOLDING ME DOWN!
YO-KAI WATCH!
WHA

FWIP
KLIKT
FWAAAASH
YO-KAI WATCH
SHINES A SPECIAL LIGHT THAT MAKES YO-KAI VISIBLE.

UGGGH
BUT ...
...YOU JUST CAN'T SWIM.

NOT KNOWING HOW TO SWIM IS NOTHING TO BE ASHAMED OF, NATE.
I DON'T THINK ANYONE WILL LAUGH AT YOU...
REALLY ?!
THEY'LL JUST THINK BADLY ABOUT YOU, QUIETLY TO THEMSELVES!
NOOOOOO!
GRAAAAH
HAVE NO FEAR! YOUR BUTLER, WHIS-PER ...
...WILL TEACH YOU TO SWIM! ♪
REAL-LY ?!

VOOOOSH
BUT I CAN'T LEARN HOW TO SWIM IN A DAY!
DON'T WORRY. ♪ I KNOW A TECHNIQUE THAT WILL HAVE YOU SWIMMING IN NO TIME.

WARM-UP EXER-CISES, HUH?
NNNGH...
STRETTCH
FIRST, STRETCH YOUR BODY!

GRRRRN...
COME ON! YOU NEED TO TWIST AT LEAST AS MUCH AS I AM!
THIS IS... AS FAR AS I CAN GO...

KRRRKT
THEN, TWIST YOUR BODY!
KEEP GOING!
HNNGH...

SQUEEEEE...
HUUUUUH?!
THEN JUST GET IN THE WATER!
SPLISH
SPLISH
...
RE-LAX...
PLOOSH

VOOOSH
... DO YOUR THING!
KRRRAKT
FWIP

JIBANYAN!
NATE CAN SUMMON YO-KAI HE'S BEFRIENDED USING THEIR YO-KAI MEDAL.

VRRRRM
...AND THE TWIST WILL POWER YOU THROUGH THE WATER!
YOU'RE LIKE A WIND-UP TOY!
ZWOOSH

C'MON! C'MON!
I CAN'T DO THAT!

THEN THERE'S NOTHING I CAN DO FOR YOU!
UGH
I'M A FAILURE!
YOU'RE GIVING UP?!

I KNOW! MAYBE HE CAN DO SOMETHING ABOUT IT...!

MEOW! ♪
FSH
FSH
JIBANYAN
WOOFH
WOOFH
JIBANYAN, I NEED TO LEARN HOW TO SWIM! HELP ME!
SPLASH!

GLUB GLUB GLUB
AAAARGH! I'M DROWNING! I'M DROWNING!
WHAAAAAA?!

LEARNING TO SWIM? LEAVE IT TO ME!
WOOOSH!
TING
NOT THAT I'VE EVER SWUM BEFORE! ♪
HUNH?
UH... NO THANKS, JIBANYAN...
I KNOW I JUST SUMMONED YOU, BUT...

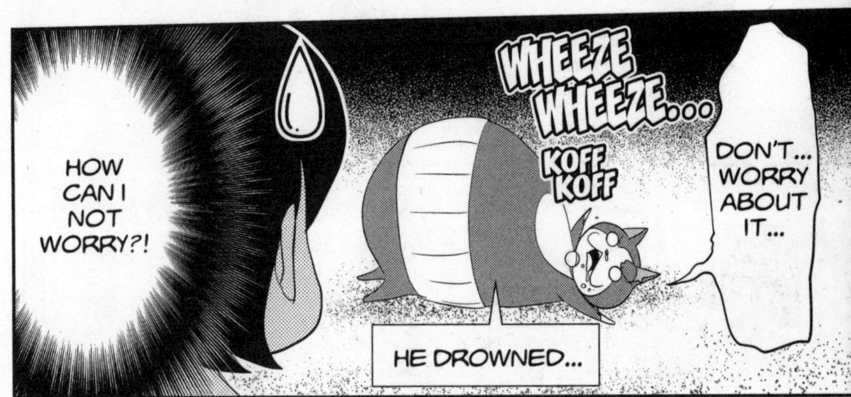
DON'T... WORRY ABOUT IT...
WHEEZE WHEEZE...
KOFF KOFF
HE DROWNED...
HOW CAN I NOT WORRY?!

ARGH, I'M DONE FOR!
THUMP...
EVERYBODY'S GOING TO THINK I SUCK!
I'LL DO SOMETHING ABOUT IT AS YOUR BUTLER!!
?

I'VE GOT AN IDEA...
PSST PSST...
WHAT?! YOU CAN DO THAT?!
W-WAIT...!

WHAAA—A
DOES THAT MEAN I'M DONE FOR THIS CHAPTER?!
THAT'S RIGHT.
THE NEXT DAY.
HAHAHA
HAHAHA
SPLISH
SPLISH
NEXT UP: NATE ADAMS!
OKAY...
YOU CAN DO IT, NATE!
AFTER YOU JUMP IN, I'LL HOLD YOU UP, SO IT LOOKS LIKE YOU'RE SWIMMING!
VOOOOSH
I'M COUNTING ON YOU, WHISPER!
GULP...
!

GLUB
HERE GOES NOTHING ...

CATCH ME, WHISPER!
VOOOOOSH

SPLOOSH
GLUB

BUT HOW DO I LOOK LIKE I'M SWIMMING?
SPLIISH
JUST LEAVE IT TO ME! ♪

HUH...?
WAIT... YOU'RE GOING TO--?
SKRRRRRNCH...

VRRRRM...
WOW, NATE!
ZWOOSH
WHAT STROKE IS HE USING?!
HA HA HA. DID YOU HEAR THAT? THEY'RE ALL SUPER IMPRES-SED!
HUH? OH ...!

THUNKT...
IDIOT ...
KRRRKT
GLUB GLUB GLUB
SORRY, I COULDN'T SEE... WHERE I WAS GOING...

NATE SUCKS.
YEAH ...
TWITCH TWITCH
EVERYTHING STRANGE IN THIS WORLD IS BECAUSE OF YO-KAI!

CHAPTER 16:
SOME THINGS ARE BETTER
LEFT UNSAID!
FEATURING DISCLOSURE YO-KAI TATTLETELL

GAAAAAH
I'M NATE ADAMS.

MURMUR
MURMUR
HA HA HA HA

DROOOL
AN ORDINARY ELEMENT-ARY SCHOOL STUDENT.

LET'S PLAY SOCCER TODAY DURING RECESS! ♪
GO PLAY BY YOUR-SELF.

OKEE DOKE. ♪
VOOOOSH
GAAAAH

MURMUR
MURMUR

THAT'S KATIE, THE CUTEST GIRL IN CLASS.
SHE'S AMAZING. ♪
EVEN HER VOICE AND THE WAY SHE TALKS IS CUTE! ♪
!?!
HEY, THAT OUT-FIT...
SHE LOOKS SUPER CUTE...
GAAAAH

WOOOOSH
...IS SOOOOO LAME!
WHAT?!
HONK!

TAKE IT EASY ON HER!
WHA
MURMUR MURMUR
AND YOU'VE GOT SOY SAUCE STAINS ON IT!
DANDRUFF TOO...
WHY ARE YOU SO MEAN?

HUH?
I HATE YOU, KATIE!
WOOOOSH
WHAT? DID I SAY SOME-THING WRONG?
BLIPT

MURMUR
MURMUR
KATIE, THAT WAS TOO HARSH.
YOU SHOULD GO APOLO-GIZE.
YOU TOOK IT WAY TOO FAR.
HOW COULD YOU SAY SOME-THING LIKE THAT?

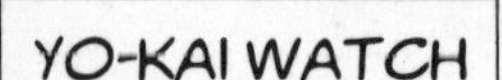
FWAAASH

KATIE WOULD NEVER SAY THOSE THINGS! IT MUST BE A YO-KAI!
YO-KAI WATCH
SHINES A SPECIAL LIGHT THAT MAKES YO-KAI VISIBLE.

THONK
HOW DARE YOU! YOU LIED TO ME!
WHAAAAT?!

WHAAAAA
YOU CAN'T PLAY SOCCER WITHOUT LEGS!
HOW'S THAT MY FAULT?!
HUH?!
THIS IS WHISPER.
I'VE HAD ENOUGH!
A YO-KAI WHO THINKS HE'S MY BUTLER.
I THINK THERE'S A YO-KAI IN HERE!
SHUFF
SHUFF
FWAASH
FWAASH
I DON'T SEE ANY...
HEY ...

WE'VE SEEN YOUR TRUE COLORS NOW, KATIE.
AS CUTE AS YOU ARE ON THE OUTSIDE, YOU'RE UGLY AND AWFUL ON THE INSIDE!
!!

BEAR! THAT'S TAKING IT WAY TOO FAR!
UGLY!
UGLY!

OH.
HUNH?

TATTLE
GUH!

THERE'S SOMETHING HANGING OFF BEAR'S CHIN!
WHAAAAA
VOOOOSH
BLIPT
HEY!
YO-KAI ARE INVISIBLE TO THE HUMAN EYE.
THAT'S TATTLETELL!! A YO-KAI THAT FORCES YOU TO SAY EXACTLY WHAT YOU'RE THINKING!
VOOOOSH
WHAT AN OBNOXIOUS YO-KAI! OKAY, I'LL CALL FOR HELP!
SHF SHF

YO-
KAI
MEDAL
!!
WOOOOSH
VOOOOSH
KRRRKT
DO
YOUR
...
THING!
CALL-
ING...
FOOOSH
JIBANYAN!
RRR
VRRRRRRN

GOOD LUCK!
I'M YOUR BIGGEST FAN! HEE HEE HEE HEE!
HEE HEE HEE

...
WAIT ... WHAT ...?

...

NOOOO!!
NOO! NOT AGAIN!
SORRY... DID I INTER-RUPT YOU...?
WHAM WHAM WHAM
RIGHT WHEN IT WAS FINALLY MY TURN AT THE NEXT HAR-MEOWNY MEET AND GREET!
OH... THEY'RE JIBANYAN'S FAVORITE MUSICIANS!
Next Harmeowny
TOO BAD ...
HUMANS CAN'T EVEN SEE YO-KAI... HOW COULD YOU MEET OR GREET THEM?
...

HE'S RIGHT!

WHAT-EVER... I DON'T FEEL LIKE HELPING YOU ANYWAY.
THUMPT
HEY!

NATE! LET'S BUTTER JIBA-NYAN UP SO HE HELPS US!
PSST... PSST...
GOOD IDEA!

I'M SORRY I KEEP SUMMONING YOU ALL THE TIME, JIBANYAN.
BUT SEEING HOW HAPPY PEOPLE GET WHEN YOU DEFEAT OTHER YO-KAI...
!

...MAKES ME FEEL HAPPY TOO!
PLUS... IF YOU DON'T FIGHT...

TATTLE
...THIS STORY ISN'T GOING ANYWHERE. STOP BEING A PAIN AND HURRY UP AND FIGHT!
HMMMMM

GRRRRRR
THERE ARE SOME THINGS YOU JUST CAN'T TAKE BACK, NATE...
WITH AS HARD AS NATE WAS PRESSING HIM... NO WONDER HE'S MAD!
HOW IS NEXT HARMEOWNY ANYWAY?
I'VE NEVER LISTENED TO THEM!
BLAH BLAH BLAH
TATTLE-TELL HAS POSSES-SED HIM!
GAAAH!

YOU'VE NEVER LISTENED TO NEXT HAR-MEOWNY?! THAT'S UNFORGIVABLE!
PAWS OF FURY!
THAT'S WHAT HE'S MAD ABOUT?
CHOOM
CHOOM
CHOOM
CHOOM
CHOO
CHOO
CHOOM
BOOSH
BOOSH
BOOSH
BOOSH
BOOSH
BOOSH

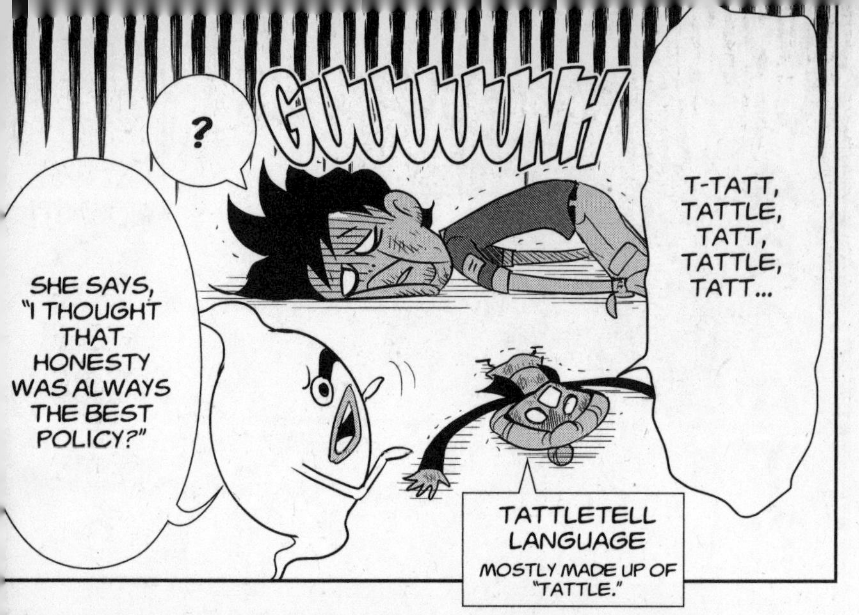
GUUUUUNH
?
T-TATT, TATTLE, TATT, TATTLE, TATT...
SHE SAYS, "I THOUGHT THAT HONESTY WAS ALWAYS THE BEST POLICY?"
TATTLETELL LANGUAGE
MOSTLY MADE UP OF "TATTLE."

WHAAAM
YOU HAVE TO RESPECT YOUR FRIENDS!
GOT THAT, NATE?!
IS BEATING THEM UP RESPECT-FUL?!
I'M... SORRY ...
OOOOOSH
TAT-TAT-TAT-TATTLE, TATTLE TAT-TAT-TAT-TAT-TAT, TAT-TAT-TAT-TAT-TAT TATTLE !!
SHUPT SHUPT
?

GAAAAAH
WHAAAAT?!
SHE WAS REALLY MOVED BY YOUR WORDS!
TATTLE. (I'VE NEVER FELT THIS WAY ABOUT ANOTHER YO-KAI BEFORE...)
TATTLE. ♡ (I LOVE YOU! ♡)
GLUMP
MEOW?! GET OFFA ME!

TATTLE. (DOES BEING WITH A FORWARD WOMAN LIKE MYSELF MAKE YOU UNCOMFORTABLE?)
TATTLE.♡ (OOOOH.♡)
THIS IS SOME KIND OF MISTAKE!
TATTLE.♪ (YOU CAN'T HIDE ANYTHING FROM ME!) ♪
PLIPT

TATTLE
BEAT IT!
TATTLE! (HOW DARE YOU!)
THIS ISN'T FAIR!
TATTLE! (FROM NOW ON, I'LL BE MORE CAREFUL ABOUT HOW I USE MY POWER.)
NATE, SHE SAYS SHE'LL GIVE YOU HER MEDAL BECAUSE YOU HELPED HER REALIZE SHE WAS WRONG!
OH!
VNNN...

I GOT ANOTHER YO-KAI MEDAL. ♪
POOPT
PROBLEM SOLVED!
NO!
IT'S NOT SOLVED JUST YET...
MURMUR
MURMUR
5-2

YO-KAI MEDAL, DO YOUR THING!
HOLD ON, KATIE! IT WASN'T YOUR FAULT!
KRRRRKT

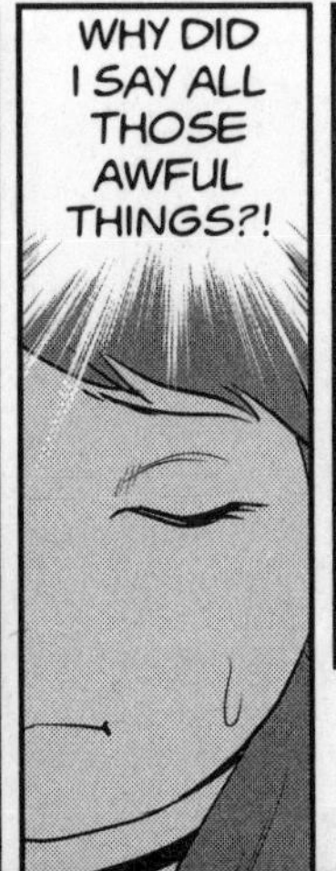
WHY DID I SAY ALL THOSE AWFUL THINGS?!

DID YOU HEAR WHAT KATIE SAID?!
SHE'S SO MEAN!
PSST
PSST
PSST

PLIPT
WHOA... I WAS REALLY MAD ABOUT SOMETHING, BUT I'VE FORGOTTEN?!
ME TOO!
ME TOO!
I FORGOT TOO!
HEY, LET'S ALL GO PLAY OUTSIDE!
YEAH, LET'S GO! LET'S GO!
LET'S GO, KATIE!
SURE! ♪
GOOD THINK-ING, NATE!
HA HA. ♪

THANKS, WAZZAT!
PIECE OF CAKE. ♪
MEMORY ERASING YO-KAI WAZZAT
A YO-KAI THAT DEVOURS MEMORIES OF THOSE WHO WEAR HIM. HE APPEARED IN VOLUME 1!

WOW... YOU'RE TURNING INTO A REAL MAN!
NO. I'M JUST HAPPY THAT KATIE IS SMILING AGAIN!
BUT DON'T YOU WANT TO TELL HER IT WAS YOU WHO HELPED HER?
WAAAUGH
WAAAAAAH! I WANT HER TO KNOW THAT I WAS THE ONE WHO SOLVED EVERYTHING!
AND I WANT HER TO HAVE A CRUSH ON ME!
TATTLE
OKAY... MAYBE HE'S NOT SO GROWN-UP YET.
NATE ADAMS'S CURRENT NUMBER OF YO-KAI FRIENDS: 16

CHAPTER 17:
INSATIABLE HUNGER!
FEATURING GLUTTONY YO-KAI HUNGORGE
CHOMP CHOMP
MUNCH MUNCH...

CHOMP CHOMP
CHOMP CRUNCH MUNCH MUNCH
MAYBE YOU SHOULD SLOW DOWN A LITTLE, NATE...
YEAH... IN FACT...
MUNCH
YOU THINK SO?
MUNCH
CHOMP CHOMP

...I THINK YOU NEED TO SLOW DOWN A LOT!
BWAAAAAH
CHOMP CHOMP
OM OM OM
MUNCH MUNCH
BUT I JUST CAN'T STOP EATING!
CRUNCH CRUNCH
KREEEAK
NATE, I'M GOING SHOP--
WHAAA
NATE'S MOM
HEH. HEH. HEH...
I CAN SUFFER THROUGH THE MESS IN YOUR BED-ROOM, BUT THE LIVING ROOM TOO...?
TING
AND EATING ALL THOSE SNACKS... YOU'RE GOING TO SPOIL YOUR APPE-TITE... BEFORE DINNER!
I'VE HAD IT...

I WANT THIS ENTIRE PLACE SPOTLESS BEFORE I GET HOME!
FOOOH!
YES MA'AM ...!
SLAM
LET'S GET STARTED, NATE.
OKAY ...

...I GUESS WE'LL HAVE TO...
RIIIP
WHAT?!

WHY ARE YOU OPENING ANOTHER PUDDING?! DIDN'T YOU LEARN YOUR LESSON?!

HEY... MAYBE I'VE BEEN POS-SESSED BY A SLACKER YO-KAI!
FWAASH..
I ONLY SEE ONE SLACKER IN THIS KITCHEN ...
HUH? WHERE'D MY PUDDING GO?!
WHA-?

PUDDING

MUNCH
FINDERS EATERS. ♪
WHAAAAAT?!
THAT'S HUNGORGE! A YO-KAI THAT TURNS PEOPLE INTO GLUTTONS!
ALL THIS FOOD IS MINE TOO. ♪
WAIT! STOP! THAT'S OUR DINNER!
FINDERS EATERS. ♪
ZLOOOSH
KRAKT
KRUNCH
CHOMPT
HEY! STOP THAT!
WOW! NATE'S GLUTTONY IS SO POWERFUL THAT HE'S FIGHTING A YO-KAI ALL ON HIS OWN!

MUNCH MUNCH MUNCH
HE GOT GOBBLED UP!
NATE'S LEG!
HUMAN? YUCK!
FWUMP
HUNH?
HE'S SO SKINNY NOW!
...
NNNGH...
URGH...
ALL THE SNACKS IN YOUR STOMACH ARE MINE TOO! ♪
I SHOVED MY TONGUE DOWN INTO YOUR STOMACH TO GET THEM!
HEH HEH HEH
THAT'S DIS-GUST-ING!
WHAT ELSE IS THERE TO EAT? ♪
OOH! ♪
SHUFF SHUFF SHUFF
HE'S GOING TO SCARF EVERY-THING WE'VE GOT IN THE FRIDGE!

CHOMP CHOMP
CHOMP
HE'S EATING THE ENTIRE FRIDGE ?!
BURRRRPT
THIS YO-KAI WILL EAT ANY-THING!
WHAA...
GRRRUUMBLE
OH NO... I'M JUST HUNGRY IS ALL! ♪
THIS CAN'T BE HEAL-THY!
NNNGH! STOMACHACHE!
URGH...
IT'S BE-CAUSE YOU ATE OUR FRIDGE!
URGH...
UNGGH...
I KNOW!
ULP ULP
HE'S COUGHING UP THE FRIDGE!

I'LL GRAB A SNACK!
THUNK!
NOW YOU'RE GOING TO EAT ALL THE FOOD INSIDE THE FRIDGE?!
CHOMP CHOMP
GLUG GLUG GLUG
GLUG GLUG GLUG
CHOMP CHOMP
CRUNCH CRUNCH
MUNCH MUNCH
EMPTY...
HE ATE EVERYTHING...

GULP...
AND NOW YOU'RE EATING THE FRIDGE AGAIN?

WHAT? DID YOU WANT A BITE?
ZWOOSH
NO NO NO! I'M GOOD!

STARTING TO?! ARE YOU KIDDING ME?! YOU ATE EVERYTHING IN THE HOUSE!
GRRRRUUUMBLE
OOOH, I'M STARTING TO GET REALLY HUNGRY.
THE TV! NOT THE AIR CONDITIONER! THAT'S OUR COFFEE TABLE! NO, STOP! PLEASE!
MUNCH MUNCH CHOMP CHOMP
NO! THE CHAIR!
MUNCH
LET'S CHOW DOWN!
I KNOW I SAID SPOTLESS...
OH...
I'M HOME! DID YOU CLEAN UP LIKE I ASKED?
...
CALL ME WHENEVER YOU'VE LOST YOUR APPETITE!
LIKE RIGHT NOW?
GRRUUMBLE
SORRY... I GOT A LITTLE GREEDY AND ATE TOO MUCH.
IF I GIVE YOU MY MEDAL, WILL YOU FORGIVE ME?
...

WHA—AAA
...BUT THIS IS RIDICULOUS!
HE ATE THE ENTIRE HOUSE!
I'M... SORRY...

NATE ADAMS'S CURRENT NUMBER OF YO-KAI FRIENDS: 17

FRIENDS

ALL RIGHT! I'M GOING TO BECOME FRIENDS WITH A YO-KAI TODAY! ♪
YEAH!
YOU CAN DO IT!

HMM ...
FWAASH
YEAH? YEAH?
Yeah? Yeah?
FWAASH

CAN YOU INTRO-DUCE ME TO SOME-ONE?
ABSO-LUTELY!

THIS IS MY FRIEND, SUZUKI. ♪
VOOOSH
HI-YA.
WHO IS THAT SUP-POSED TO BE?!
I MEANT A YO-KAI!

ORIGINALLY PRINTED WITH THE NINTENDO 3DS GAME, YO-KAI WATCH.

CHAPTER 18: THE PERFECT TEAM?!

FEATURING POWERFUL YO-KAI GORUMA

NATE! DID YOU HEAR?!
HEAR WHAT?

THIS CHAPTER ONLY HAS EIGHT PAGES!
REALLY? JUST EIGHT PAGES?

GRRRAAAAH!
POWERFUL YO-KAI GORUMA
WHY DID THEY HAVE TO INTRODUCE SUCH A CRAZY-LOOKING YO-KAI?!
WE CAN'T BEAT THIS THING IN EIGHT PAGES!
NATE, I HAVE SOME BACK-GROUND ON HIM. MAYBE IT'LL HELP?
PER-FECT! TELL ME!
CLOMP
CLOMP
CLOMP
A HUMAN WHO CAN ACTUALLY SEE ME?! I'M GOING TO CLOBBER YOU!
HE'S JUST TRY-ING TO PICK A FIGHT!
BUT WHY?!
BE-CAUSE I FEEL LIKE IT!

APPARENTLY, HE'S STRONG ENOUGH TO CRUSH A CAR! ♪
AND THAT'S ALL I'VE GOT...
THAT DOESN'T HELP AT ALL! IT JUST MAKES ME MORE INTI-MIDATED!

WELL... GOOD LUCK, JIBANYAN!
TUMP
ARE YOU KIDDING?! I DON'T WANT TO FIGHT THAT THING!

QUIT YOUR YAMMER-ING! HERE I COME!

LET'S TRY THIS ...
YO-KAI MED-AL!
FWIP
FWIP
FWIP FWIP FWIP
TEKT
DO YOUR ...
KRRRKT

... THING!
CALL-ING...
NN
NN
NN
NN
NN
NN

TATTLE-TELL!!
VRRRN...
TATTLE!
TATTLE
OH NO!
HUNH?
TING!
SHE HAS A CRUSH ON JIBANYAN!
NNGH...
WHY DID YOU HAVE TO SUMMON HER?!
SHE'S OBVIOUSLY NO MATCH FOR IT!
BECAUSE WE'RE GOING TO FIGHT HIM AS A TEAM!
GET READY, JIBANYAN!
MEOW.
I'M COUNTING ON YOU! TATTLE-TELL!!
BOING BOING BOING
TATTLE!
?
HEY...
WHAT'S YOUR WEAKNESS?
WELL, IT'S NOTHING SPECIAL, BUT...

...EVERY MAN'S WEAKNESS IS HIS--
HIYAAAAH!
THUNGK!!
AIYEEEEEEEE!

CHUNGK
PAWS OF FURY!
CHUNGK CHUNGK
GAAAAH!
YOU'RE TAKING IT TOO FAR!
WHAAAA...

GAAAAAH
TWITCH TWITCH...
WE ONLY NEEDED SIX PAGES TO BEAT HIM!

VNN...

YOU WIN ...
YOU'VE DE-FEATED ME, SO I WILL NOW SWEAR ALLE-GIANCE TO YOU, NATE ADAMS.
BOING BOING
THERE'S NO NEED FOR ALL THAT- JUST BE MY FRIEND!

POP
I GOT ANOTHER YO-KAI MEDAL! ♪
IT WAS SO SMART OF YOU TO USE TATTLETELL TO LEARN HIS WEAKNESS! ♪
WE CAN START USING THIS STRATEGY ALL THE TIME!
TATTLE. ♪
...
RIGHT, JIBANYAN?
I CAN FIGHT MY OWN BATTLES, THANK YOU!
COME ON! YOU TWO WORK SO WELL TOGETHER!
RIGHT, TATTLETELL?
...

AHHHHH!
SHE'S GETTING THE WRONG IDEA AGAIN!

TATTLE. ♡
(WE'RE THE PERFECT TEAM!♡)
PLIP

SUMMON ME WITH TATTLETELL ONE MORE TIME AND I'LL NEVER HELP YOU AGAIN!
GRRRAAAAAH!
TAT-TATTLE! ♡
(I WON'T DO ANYTHING UNLESS IT'S WITH MY SWEET JIBANYAN!♡)
WHAAAAAT?!

NATE ADAMS'S CURRENT NUMBER OF YO-KAI FRIENDS: 18

CHAPTER 19: THE MANJIMUTT BITES!

FEATURING GROVELING YO-KAI MANJIMUTT

HEY, WHISPER! LET'S GO FOR A WALK! ♪
WHISSS! ♪
I'M NATE ADAMS.

VOO—OSH
WHAT A BEAUTIFUL DAY!
IT SURE IS!
KACHINK
SHUFF SHUFF
AN ORDINARY ELEMENTARY SCHOOL STUDENT.

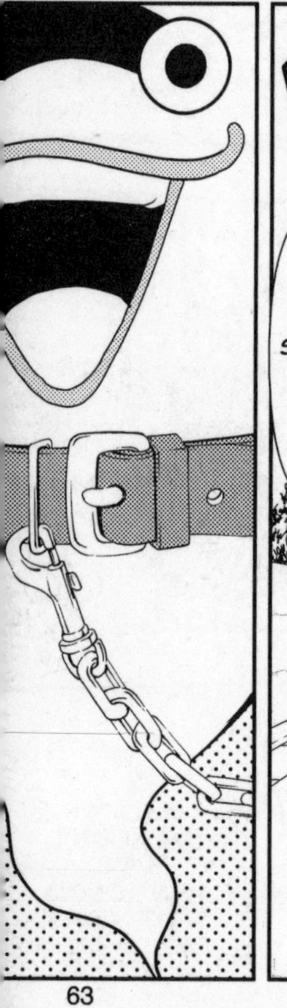

WAIT A MINUTE!
HEEEEEY!
WHY AM I WEARING A COLLAR AND LEASH?!
SWAPT
THIS IS WHISPER.
I'VE ALWAYS WANTED A DOG!
NNNGH...
BUT THAT DOESN'T MEAN YOU GET TO TREAT ME LIKE ONE!
OWW!
OH NO... ARE YOU JEAL-OUS?
HEE HEE
GAAAAH!
JEAL-OUS?! NO!

I'M SORRY. I SHOULDN'T HAVE MENTIONED THAT TO MY PET YO-KAI...
SORRY.
WHA AAA
WHAAAAA
I'M YOUR PET?!
A YO-KAI WHO THINK HE'S MY BUTLER.

I'M...A PET... NOTHING MORE... THAN A PET?!
THERE'S SUPPOSED TO BE A TALKING DOG IN THIS NEIGHBORHOOD SOMEWHERE.
!

WHAT? REALLY?!

LET'S GO FIND IT!
YEEEEAH!
A TALKING DOG ...

IT'D BE THE PERFECT PET! ♡
I'M JUST A PRECIOUS LITTLE DOGGIE.
AWWWW
WILL YOU BE MY OWNER?
WHAT ARE YOU TALKING ABOUT? IT'S OBVIOUSLY A YO-KAI!
REALLY?

WELL, IN THAT CASE, I'LL JUST FIND IT AND TAKE IT HOME WITH ME ANYWAY! ♪
FWAAASH
HE THINKS WE'RE JUST PETS...

!
GAAAAAAH!
VOOOOOSH

IT'S SOME OLD FREAK! HE'S AFTER US!
AHHHH!
?!
WAIT! YOU! COME BACK HERE!

VOOOOSH
IT IS SOME OLD FREAK!
WHO ARE YOU CALLING AN OLD FREAK?!
WHAAAAA

HUFF HUFF
WHY DO YOU ALL THINK I'M SOME KIND OF FREAK?!
YOU'RE A MIDDLE-AGED MAN DRESSED UP LIKE A DOG!

NO! I'M A DOG WITH THE FACE OF A MIDDLE-AGED MAN!
TAKE A GOOD LOOK!
THEN THAT MAKES YOU A MONSTER!

A MON-STER ...?!
GRRAW...

TUMP TUMP
TUMP TUMP
I KNEW IT! I'M DONE FOR!!
GAAAH! HE CALLED ME A MONSTER!
NOOOOO!
WHAT ARE YOU DOING?! WHAT'S WRONG WITH YOU?!
THIS IS MANJI-MUTT...
HE'S AN EXTREMELY SELF-CONSCIOUS YO-KAI.
WHY CAN I SEE HIM EVEN WITHOUT MY YO-KAI WATCH?
SOME YO-KAI ARE SO CLUMSY THAT ANYONE CAN SEE THEM.
THUNGK
OH... SO HE'S A KLUTZ.
DID YOU JUST CALL ME KLUTZ?!

I'M A MONSTER AND A KLUTZ! I SHOULD BE ASHAMED OF MYSELF!
TUMP TUMP
TUMP TUMP
KNOCK IT OFF FOR A MINUTE!
GROVELING YO-KAI
MANJIMUTT

HEFH HEFH BECAUSE I LOOK LIKE THIS... NO DOG WANTS TO BE MY FRIEND, AND NO HUMAN WANTS TO BE MY OWNER.
THUNGK...
YOU'VE JUST HAD A RUN OF BAD LUCK. I'M SURE YOU'LL FIND SOME FRIENDS SOON! ♪

WHAT...? YOU MEAN IT'S NOT BECAUSE OF HOW I LOOK?
HUUNH...
I... YEAH, SURE!

THEN YOU'LL LET ME BECOME YOUR PET?!
EEEEEE
SORRY, I'M NOT ALLOWED TO HAVE ANY PETS...
MY MOM'S SUPER STRICT...
YOU JUST SAID YOU ALWAYS WANTED A DOG!

YOU'RE SURE IT'S NOT BECAUSE OF HOW I LOOK?
HMMMM...
Y-Y-YEAH...

HMMMMM

SO YOU DON'T THINK I LOOK WEIRD?
HMMMMM
NO... NOT AT ALL. YOU'RE JUST UNIQUE!

HMMMMM
REALLY? SERIOUSLY? ARE YOU SURE?

EXCELLENT! I THINK WE'RE GOING TO BE GREAT FRIENDS! ♪
AHHHH
FRIENDS...? YEAH... SURE! ♪
YOU GOT IT! ♪

OKAY THEN...

CREEPY SUPERBITE!
CHOMP
GAAAAAH! WHY DID YOU DO THAT?!

YOU REA-LLY...
...DON'T THINK I LOOK WEIRD?
GEEZ, JUST TRUST ME...

...I TOTALLY DON'T!
WHAAA
NATE?!
HUUNH?!

WHAT HAPPENED TO ME?!
AAAAARGH!
EVERY-ONE I BITE TURNS INTO A MANJI-MUTT TOO!
SINCE YOU DON'T THINK IT'S WEIRD, IT'S NO BIG DEAL, RIGHT?
NOW WE'RE FRIENDS AND WE LOOK ALIKE TOO!

HMMM
NATE!
SEE! SEE! YOU WERE LYING TO ME ALL ALONG, WEREN'T YOU?!
WHAAAAA?! I DON'T WANT TO GO AROUND LOOKING LIKE THIS!
THERE, THERE. GOOD BOY! ♪
SHAKE HANDS!
THWEE THWEE
DON'T TREAT ME LIKE A DOG!
CALM DOWN NOW.
HOW CAN I CALM DOWN?!
CH
OMP
GAAAAH! OWWWWW!
YOU DIDN'T HAVE TO BITE ME...!
OWW...

WHA——AAA
LET'S JUST SETTLE DOWN AND THINK OF A WAY OUT OF THIS!
...

NOOOO!
AAAARGH!
CALM DOWN!

HOW CAN I CALM DOWN?!
NOW YOU KNOW HOW I FEEL!
WOW... I REALLY DO LOOK WEIRD.

SHLUMPF
WHAT'S WRONG WITH YOU NOW?!

IF WE BEAT HIM UP, IT WILL PROBABLY REMOVE THE CURSE!
GOOD IDEA!
YO-KAI MED-AL!
KRRRKT
DO YOUR THING!
CALL-ING...
VNNNNNN
JIBA-NYAN!

KA-FWUMPT
HUNH?
MUNCH MUNCH
WHAT HAP-PENED TO YOU?!
I ALWAYS GAIN WEIGHT AROUND THE HOLIDAY SEASON... TOO MUCH GOOD FOOD!
NNGH... I CAN'T STAND UP...!
HUFF HUFF
SHEFF SHEFF
HE'S... HE'S A GIANT BALL!
WELL ...

AT LEAST I STILL LOOK BETTER THAN YOU TWO!
YOU BOTH LOOK RIDICULOUS!
WHAAAA
SIGH...

THAT YO-KAI CURSED US! BEAT HIM UP AND WE'LL GO BACK TO NORMAL! PLEASE, JIBA-NYAN!
BUT I... DON'T REALLY WANT TO MOVE RIGHT NOW.
I KNOW!
NNGH NNGH

I'LL CRUSH YOU FLAT!
WUB WUB WUB
HE'S SO LAZY!
GAAAAAAH!
THOOM
YEAH! ♪

HELP ME!
NNGH NNGH NNGH
HE'S STUCK IN THE GUTTER!
THAT'S THE BEST YOU CAN DO?!
...

OOOOOOOO!
YES! YES! YES!
?!
WHAT ?!

THERE'S A CAT WHO'S EVEN UGLIER THAN ME!
AHHHH...
AT LEAST MY LIFE IS BETTER THAN HIS! ♪
HE FEELS BETTER NOW THAT HE'S SEEN SOMEONE EVEN WORSE OFF!
HEY! THAT'S NOT FUNNY! TIME FOR...

PAWS OF FURY !!
FEET VERSION!
CHOOM CHOOM
CHOOM CHOOM CHOOM
GRAAAAAAAH!
SHUPT
NOW DO YOU SEE ...
...HOW POWER-FUL I AM?!
VOOOSH

YES...
...
THUMPT...
SORRY! I COULDN'T SEE WHO I WAS ATTACK-ING!
...
TWITCH TWITCH...
TWITCH TWITCH...
WHAAAA...

AND HE'S SO STUPID TOO! I'M SO MUCH BETTER THAN HIM. ♪
THANK YOU...!
MAYBE LIFE ISN'T SO BAD AFTER ALL!
THIS GUY'S HOPE-LESS...

HOW COULD YOU DO THIS TO NATE AND WHIS-PER?!
YOU'RE THE ONE WHO BEAT THEM UP!
WHAAA?!
I'LL NEVER FOR-GIVE YOU!

PAWS OF FURY!
CHOOM
CHOOM
CHOOM CHOOM

HE'S SO FAT HE CAN'T EVEN REACH MANJI-MUTT...!
FOOFH FOOFH FOOFH
WHAAAA

HEFH, HEFH ...
WHEEZE
WHEEZE
JUST...A MINUTE... NEED...A QUICK... BREAK...
...

MUNCH MUNCH MUNCH
NOW YOU'RE JUST HAVING A SNACK?!
DRIED BONITO CHIPS
HUUUH?!

GRRR RRRR
I'LL TURN YOU INTO A DOG TOO!

NNNGH
I HAVE NO CHOICE!

VOOOOSH
WHAAAAT?!
HUUUNH?!
HE'S RUN-NING AWAY!
TUMP

MRRRRAOW!
THOOM
...

SO VERY STUPID ...
GUUUH...
HUNH?

SPROOOOING
GAAAAH!
THUN
GKT

FLUMPT...

WE DID IT!
BUT WE HAVEN'T TURNED BACK!
WHAT?! YOU'RE RIGHT!
ARE WE STUCK LIKE THIS FOR-EVER ?!

LIKE THIS... FOR-EVER ...

TWITCH TWITCH TWITCH
MAN... IT ALWAYS ENDS UP LIKE THIS...
AND IT'S ALL BE-CAUSE OF HOW I LOOK.

IF I DIDN'T LOOK LIKE THIS, I'D BE A CHEERFUL, HAPPY GUY WITH A TON OF FRIENDS.
!

IF YOU WANT... WE COULD BE YOUR FRIENDS! ♪
...

I DON'T WANT YOUR SYMPATHY.

IT'S NOT SYMPATHY! WE LOOK THE SAME NOW ANYWAY.

WE'RE ALL IN THIS TOGETHER NOW, SO LET'S HELP EACH OTHER THE BEST WE CAN! ♪
!!

NATE, YOU REALLY NEED TO BE HONEST WITH HIM IF YOU WANT HIM TO BELIEVE YOU.
WHAT? REALLY?

I HAVE BEEN LIED TO MY ENTIRE LIFE... SO I CAN ALWAYS TELL...
BUT HIS EYES...

...HE'S TELLING THE TRUTH!

?

I DIDN'T EXPECT YOU TO ACCEPT YOUR NEW LOOK SO EASILY.
SHUFF SHUFF

DRINK THIS.
?

HOO-RAY! ♪
YEEEAAH
WOO-HOO!
A POTION THAT WILL TURN US BACK?!

WE CAN STILL BE FRIENDS.
NO, IT'S OKAY. YOU'RE AN HONEST GUY.

HEH.

OH, I'M SOR-RY!
NATE!

HOORAY! I GOT ANOTHER YO-KAI MEDAL! ♪
POPT

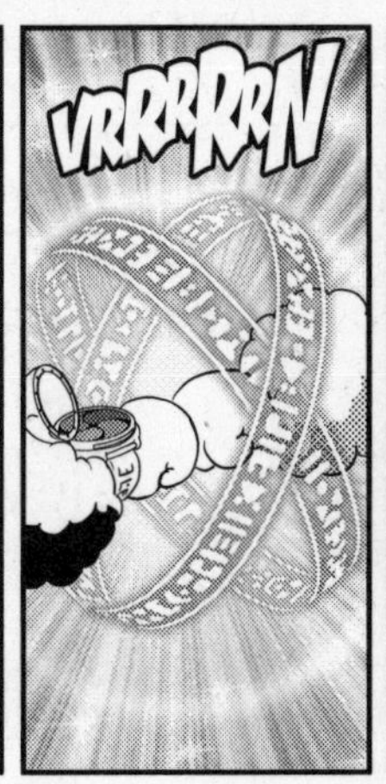
VRRRRRN

GLUG GLUG
SHUPT
WE'RE BACK TO NOR-MAL! ♪

I'M SO GRATE-FUL!

THANKS TO YOU, I'VE GAINED SOME CONFI-DENCE IN MYSELF!

I'LL TRY TO BE MORE POSITIVE FROM NOW ON. SO LONG!
BYE!

HELLO! LOVELY DAY WE'RE HAVING!
AIIIIII EEE! A MON-STER!

AWWW...
SIIIIGH
VOOOOOSH
EEEEE!
HE'S ALREADY DEPRES-SED AGAIN!

THANKS SO MUCH, JIBA-NYAN.
BUT YOU REALLY SHOULDN'T EAT SO MUCH!
YOU'RE RIGHT. I'LL GO ON A DIET...

NATE ADAMS'S CURRENT NUMBER OF YO-KAI FRIENDS: 19

YO-KAI.
CREATURES THAT BRING PEOPLE LUCK... BOTH GOOD AND BAD...
MOST UNEXPLAINABLE THINGS IN THE WORLD ARE ACTUALLY THEIR DOING!

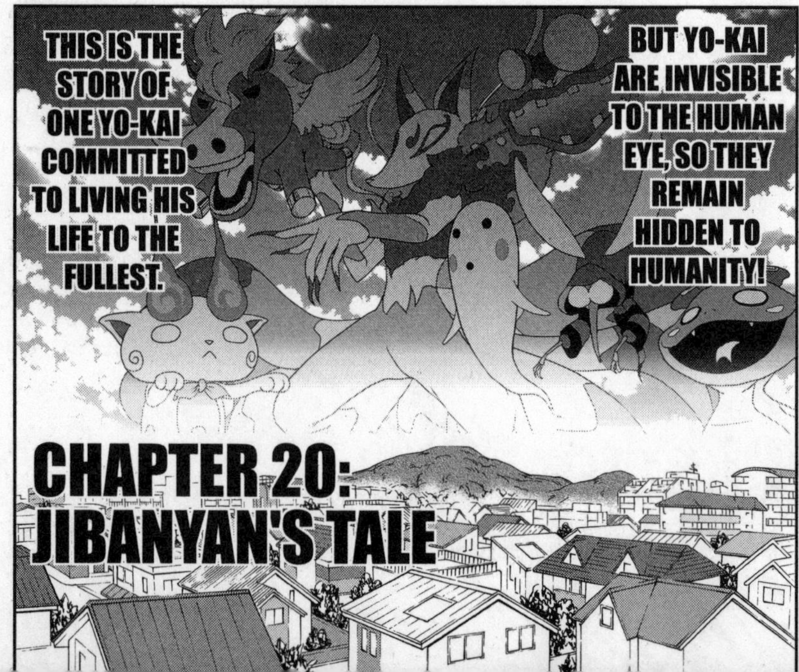
BUT YO-KAI ARE INVISIBLE TO THE HUMAN EYE, SO THEY REMAIN HIDDEN TO HUMANITY!
THIS IS THE STORY OF ONE YO-KAI COMMITTED TO LIVING HIS LIFE TO THE FULLEST.
CHAPTER 20: JIBANYAN'S TALE

Chapter 20: JIBANYAN'S TALE

CHOOM
CH
CHO

OM NOM NOM
FRESH FISH FOR SALE! ♪
STEP RIGHT UP FOR THE FRESHEST FISH IN TOWN! ♪
Best
FRESH
The Fish Place
MUNCH MUNCH
CHOMP CHOMP
SHUFF SHUFF SHUFF

RESH
The Fish Place
THE FISH HAVE ALL DISAP- PEARED!
I'LL TAKE THREE MACK- ERELS PLEASE!
COMING RIGHT UP!
WHAAA
KRKT KRKT
TUMP TUMP
YO-KAI NOTE 1: MISSING ITEMS ARE A CLASSIC SIGN OF YO-KAI MISCHIEF!
MY NAME IS JIBANYAN. I'M A YO-KAI.
BUUURP
SINCE THE HUMANS CAN'T SEE ME, I GET TO EAT AS MUCH AS I WANT!
BUT...

VOOOSH
THUNGK!
ARRRRGH!
...THIS TENDS TO HAPPEN A LOT.

SHUNGK
UNGH!
THUMPT
WHOOOA! WHAT TRIPPED ME?!
IN THE OLD DAYS...

YO-KAI NOTE 2: EVER TRIP OVER NOTHING? THAT'S A YO-KAI'S DOING!

...I WAS JUST AN ORDINARY CAT.
THEN I GOT HIT BY A CAR...
MNGH...
MNGH...
BUT!
GRRRRRRN

TA-DAH
I WAS CONSUMED WITH SO MUCH RESENTMENT AND FRUSTRATION THAT I RETURNED AS A YO-KAI!
NOW IT'S MY DREAM TO BECOME STRONG ENOUGH TO DESTROY THE THING THAT TOOK MY LIFE... A CAR!

HMMM
TO TRAIN MYSELF, I FIGHT EVERY CAR I SEE!
VROOOM...
A SMALL CAR! I'M SURE I CAN TAKE IT!
HOP!

PAWS OF FURY!
CHOOM CHOOM CHOOM CHOOM CHOOM
CHOOM CHOOM CHOOM...
HUNH?

RUUUU
TUNK TUNK TUNK
WHAAAAAAT?!
M-M-BLE
VOOOOOM
THUNGK
MRRAAAAOW!
NNGH NNGH
VROOOOOM
NOT... SO FAST! I'M NOT... DONE YET!
NNNGHH...
MEEEEEOW!

MRRRRAAAAOW!
THUMPT
SQUEE SQUEE

THIS IS THE STORY OF ONE YO-KAI COMMITTED TO LIVING HIS LIFE TO THE FULLEST.
TWITCH TWITCH
ONE DAY... I'LL BE ABLE... TO DE-FEAT... A CAR...!
TWITCH TWITCH

JIBANYAN

FROM THE NINTENDO 3DS GAME, YO-KAI WATCH.

CHAPTER 21: HOW TO FIGHT AN INVISIBLE ENEMY!

FEATURING LOW PROFILE YO-KAI BLANDON

GRAAAAAAAAH!
AAAAAAAAAAAA!
EEEEEE

HUNH?!
HUNH?!
AM I STILL IMPORTANT? DOES IT EVEN MATTER THAT I'M HERE? WHAT DO YOU THINK?!
JIBANYAN GETS ALL THE GOOD SCENES! NATE, DO I EVEN HELP YOU AT ALL ANYMORE?!
HUNH?!

WAAAAAH
PLEASE, GIVE ME A CHANCE TO SHOW HOW VALUABLE I AM! PLEASE! JUST TELL ME WHAT I HAVE TO DO!
OKAY. FOR START-ERS...

SHUT UP.
YOU'RE TOO LOUD...
SHUPT
YES SIR! WHEN IT COMES TO SHUTTING UP, THERE'S NO ONE BETTER THAN ME! I'M THE BEST AT SHUTTING UP! AFTER ALL, I'M NATURALLY QUIET RESERVED--
SHUT UP!

BYE, NATE.
CHATTER
CHATTER CHATTER
SHUTTING UP IS ACTUALLY QUITE EASY--
SO ANNOYING!
WHEN YOU GET DOWN TO IT...
BYE!
LATER!

AM I JUST HEARING THINGS?

?
HUNH? WHO SAID THAT?

OH! HEY, ALEX. LONG TIME NO SEE...
LONG TIME NO SEE? BUT I'M HERE EVERY DAY!

GAAAH!
SHUFF...
BYE, NATE.

HE DOESN'T DO OR SAY MUCH IN CLASS, SO I NEVER REALLY NOTICE HIM...
...
SHUFF...
BYE.

RRRRRRR...
THE YO-KAI HIMSELF IS VERY INCON-SPICUOUS, SO IF YOU MISS HIM...

I JUST NOTICED ALEX, SO THE YO-KAI MUST HAVE ALREADY LEFT HIM.
HE POS-SESSES PEOPLE WITHOUT BEING NOTICED, THEN MAKES THEM UNASSUMING AND INCON-SPICUOUS!

WHAT? WHERE?!
THAT'S BECAUSE HE'S BEING POS-SESSED BY A YO-KAI THAT MAKES HIM FORGET-TABLE!
FSSSSH!!
!

VOOOOSH
HE'S STANDING RIGHT NEXT TO YOU...
...YOU'LL NEVER BE ABLE TO SPOT HIM AGAIN!

WHAAA?!
HUNH?! I DIDN'T NOTICE YOU BECAUSE YOU'RE SO UNASSUM-ING!

NOOOOOO!
WHY CAN THAT HUMAN SEE ME?!
SOR-RY.

HUH? HE DISAP-PEARED AGAIN!
FWAASH
YOU JUST CAN'T SEE HIM BECAUSE HE'S SO INCON-SPICUOUS!

NAAAAH... I WAS JUST HIDING THIS TIME. ♪
TA-DAAAH! I'M RIGHT OVER HERE!
SHUPT
WHAT IS HE DOING?!

INCON-SPICUOUS, LOW PROFILE YO-KAI BLAN-DON...
YEAH, YEAH, YEAH!
...IS ON THE SCENE!
LOW-PROFILE YO-KAI BLANDON
HE HAS A LOW PROFILE, BUT HE'S STILL A SHOW-OFF...

DON'T COME NEAR ME!
HA HA HA. ♪ DON'T WORRY! ♪ I'M NOT GOING TO POSSESS YOU...
BUT ...
I'M ALREADY HAVING TROUBLE WITH PEOPLE FORGETTING ABOUT ME!
SHUFFF

...I AM GOING TO KILL YOU!
WHAT?!
HEH HEH HEH... I LIVE A SIMPLE, RECLUSIVE LIFE. BUT SINCE YOU NOTICED ME, I'VE BEEN EXPOSED...
SCHING
...NOW I'LL ELIMINATE YOU BOTH!
TUMP TUMP
UHH... EXCUSE ME... ARE YOU EVEN LISTENING TO ME?

OH YEAH! I FORGOT ABOUT THE YO-KAI!
WOOOSH
I TOTALLY FORGOT YOU WERE THERE!
ARE YOU KIDDING ME?!
WHAAA?!
AM I THAT FORGETTABLE?! EVEN WHEN I'M TRYING TO KILL YOU?!
REGARDLESS, ANYONE WHO SEES A NINJA MUST DIE!
HUFF HUFF
BUT YOU'RE THE ONE WHO REVEALED YOURSELF TO US!

NATE! RUN!
DIE!
CALLING ...
VNNN NOOO
KRRRKT
TIIING
I'LL SHOW YOU ...
CADIN!
GIVE HIM A TASTE OF HIS OWN MEDICINE!

ZU!
WHAT?! HE THREW A NINJA STAR AT CADIN'S HEAD!
SHUNGKT
ISH
NO FAIR!
CADIN!
MNNGH...
FWUMPT
SHUP
THUNGK

HUUUH?! WHAT'S GOING ON?!
VOOOSH
I FORGOT. HE TURNED INTO A ZOMBIE...!
A ZOMBIE?!
SHUDDER
I'LL CHOP YOU INTO PIECES SO SMALL YOU'LL NEVER PUT THEM BACK TOGETHER!

VWOOOSH
NINJA CLONES!
MY CLONES WILL MAKE SHORT WORK OF YOU!
AND THEN I'LL DEAL WITH YOU TWO!
!
NATE! CADIN CAN'T HANDLE THEM ALL ON HIS OWN!
YOU'RE RIGHT!
CALL-ING...
VNNNN...

BAAM
NOKO
(LUCKY YO-KAI)
WAZZAT
(MEMORY EATING YO-KAI)
MOCHISMO
(RICE CAKE YO-KAI)

VOO
DAIZ
(SPACED-OUT YO-KAI)

OOSH
NEGASUS
(TROUBLE YO-KAI)

AND JIBA-NYAN!

TATTLE
TATTLE
TATTLE
TATTLETELL
(DISCLOSURE YO-KAI)

FWUMPT
TWITCH TWITCH
HUUUUH?!
WHAT HAPPENED?!
I WASN'T LOOKING AND GOT RUN OVER BY A TRICYCLE...
THUMPT
SQUEE SQUEE
YOU HAVE TO PAY BETTER ATTENTION!
JIBANYAN

COME ON, GUYS! I NEED YOU TO TEACH THAT YO-KAI A LESSON!
VOOSH VOOSH
VOOSH
YOU GOT IT, NATE!

RRRRRRR—
WE'LL TAKE CARE OF HIM!
GAAAAAH!

THUNGK THUNGK
TAKE THAT, ZOMBIE YO-KAI!
STOP! NO! HE'S ON OUR SIDE!
M-I-I-I...

SWAP
CHOOM
CHOOM
THOOM
CHOMP
THUNGK

ATTACKING THE CLONES ISN'T GETTING US ANYWHERE!
WE HAVE TO FIND THE REAL BLANDON!
BUT WHICH ONE IS HE?!

HE MUST BE KEEPING A LOW PROFILE AND HIDING FROM US!
HOW DO WE FIGURE OUT WHERE HE IS?!

BOO—IING
TATTLE! (LEAVE IT TO ME!!)

TATTLE
THAT'S HIM!
DON'T TELL THEM!!
TATTLE! (WHO'S THE REAL BLAN-DON?!)
SHUPT
AHA!
ANYONE POSSESSED BY TATTLETELL WILL SPEAK THE TRUTH.

VOOO OSH
SO IT'S YOU!
NNGH ...!

FWUMPT
MORE CLONES !
!!!

TATTLE
IT'S HIM!
MORE CLONES !
HEY!

HE'S JUST GOING TO KEEP CREA-TING MORE AND MORE CLONES. WE HAVE TO STOP HIM...
HERE ...
VOOOSH
!

WOOOOSH
AL-LOW ME!

DON'T MAKE HIM FORGET WHO HE IS! IT'LL MAKE THINGS MORE CONFUSING!
I CAN'T REMEMBER.
WHAT? I'M THE REAL ONE? AM I REALLY?
ANYONE WHO WEARS WAZZAT LOSES THEIR MEMORY.

NOW THEY'RE ALL JUST LYING TO US! STOP IT!
IT'S ME!
IT'S ME!
IT'S ME!
NO, I'M THE REAL BLANDON!
IT'S ME! NO, ME! ME!
I'M THE REAL BLANDON.
WHEN NEGASUS IS NEARBY, YOU'RE TEMPTED TO CAUSE TROUBLE.

THANKS, NEGASUS!
LEAVE IT TO ME! I'LL MAKE HIM TELL THE TRUTH!
CLIP-CLOP

NOOOO! HE'S POSSESSED BY DAIZ!
DAAAZE...
ANYONE POSSESSED BY DAIZ WILL SPACE OUT.

WHAAA...
...
THAT ONE HASN'T SAID ANYTHING YET!
IT MUST BE HIM!

DON'T WORRY, THE REAL ONE IS...

...
WHAT ARE WE GOING TO DO, NATE?

...HIM!
!!
HOW CAN YOU TELL?!
I'VE GOT A HUNCH. ♪
AH
HA!
WHAAAAT?! YOU'RE JUST GUESSING ?!
HOW DID YOU KNOW?! I WAS HIDDEN PERFECTLY !!
YOOOOSH
YOUR HUNCH WAS RIGHT?! NO WAY!
WHAAAA

NOW'S MY CHANCE!
KRA-THOOM
UNNNGH!
THUNGGGKT
TWITCH TWITCH
POP POP
THE CLONES ARE DISAP-PEARING... I GUESS IT *WAS* THE REAL BLANDON!
WAS IT REALLY JUST A HUNCH?
HA HA. ♪

IT'S ALL THANKS TO HIM!
SQUEEE. ♪
NOKO!
SO THAT'S WHY YOU GUESSED RIGHT!
ANYONE NEAR NOKO BECOMES LUCKY.

HEH HEH HEH...
!
WHAT'S SO FUNNY?

OH NO... IT'S JUST THAT I HAVE SPENT SO LONG ESCAPING PEOPLE'S NOTICE...
...THAT IT'S BEEN A WHILE SINCE I ACTUAL-LY USED MY NINJU-TSU...

I HAD FUN!
HEH HEH.
...

I WAS VERY LONELY AND WANTED OTHER PEOPLE TO FEEL THE SAME WAY I DID.
I'M SORRY...
WELL...

WHY DON'T YOU BECOME FRIENDS WITH US?!
!!!
REALLY ?
OF COURSE!

VMMN...
POPT
HOORAY! ♪ I GOT ANOTHER YO-KAI MEDAL! ♪

NATE ADAMS'S CURRENT NUMBER OF YO-KAI FRIENDS: 20.

CHAPTER 22:
SPA BATTLE OVERFLOW!
FEATURING GYM LOVER YO-KAI SPROINK
BRRRR... IT'S FREEZ-ING...
IT'S WINTER ALREADY ?!
SHUDDER SHUDDER
TREMBLE TREMBLE
OOH...! A GYM! ♪
I'LL TAKE A QUICK DIP TO WARM UP! ♪
BATH
HUMANS CAN'T SEE ME, SO I CAN USE THE SPA AS MUCH AS I WANT! ♪
WOMEN
TUMP TUMP
HUNH?

EMPTY HOUSE! LUCKY ME! ♪
PSSSH—HHH
BOING!
SPLOOSH

FSS-SSH

AIYEEEEEEEE!
WHY IS THE WATER SO HOT?!
SPLOOSH
RRRRRRR...

HA HA HA HA HA HA HA
BECAUSE I'M HEATING IT UP! ♪

HA HA HA HA HA HA
ARE YOU EVEN LISTENING TO ME?!

A YO-KAI THAT LIVES IN GYMS!
YOU'RE SPROINK!

SPLASH
YOW-WWW! HOT!

GAAAAAH! STOP BREATHING FIRE EVERY-WHERE!
FWOOOOSH
HUH?

PSSSSS...
HUFF HUFF
AIIIIIIEEE! THIS ONE'S HOT TOO!
SPLOOSH
NOW I KNOW WHY NO ONE'S HERE... YOU'RE MAKING IT TOO HOT!
OINK! A LUKE-WARM SPA ISN'T EVEN A SPA AT ALL!
YOU'RE MAKING IT TOO HOT FOR PEOPLE TO ENJOY! KNOCK IT OFF!
NEVER! I REFUSE TO GIVE UP MY HOT SPAS!
THEN I'LL BEAT THE SNOT OUT OF YOU AND ADD WATER TO COOL IT DOWN!

PAWS OF FURY!!
CHOOM
CHOOM
CHOOM
CHOOM
SPAAASH!!
HAHAHAHA
OINK!
KRUNCH
AAAAARGH!
HE'S USING HIS FLAMES TO FLY!
WHAAT?!
...
FZZT...

F-WOOOSH
WHAAAT?! HIS CLOTHES CAUGHT FIRE!
AIIEEE! HELP ME!

HEY! WHAT ARE YOU DOING?! HELP ME!
AHHHHHH
THAT'S IT... ♪ NOW THE WATER'S JUUUUUST FINE! ♪
USE THE BATH WATER TO PUT OUT THE FIRE!
HURRY!!
SPLOOOSH
HUP!

GLUB
GLUB GLUB
SLURRP SLURRP
GLUB
OH, BRO-THER...

NNNNNGH
BUUUUU-RRRRP! I'M STUFFED ...
GAAAAAH!
YOU'RE WASTING TIME DRINK-ING!
HURRY UP AND HELP ME!
NNNGH
EXTIN-GUISH!
SPLOOOOOSH
SHWAAASH
LET THIS BE A LESSON TO NEVER USE FIRE IN A SPA AGAIN!
FSSSH FSSSH
THUNGKT
YOU'RE RIGHT... I'M SORRY ...
NOW IT'S TIME TO RELAX WITH A NICE, HOT SPA! ♪
BOING

THUNCK!
MRRRR-AAAOW!
I EMPTIED ALL THE WATER TO PUT THE FIRE OUT!
MAYBE IT'S A YO-KAI MAKING YOUR SPA TOO HOT AND LETTING THE WATER RUN OUT!

CHAPTER 23: JIBANYAN'S FLIGHT DREAM!

FEATURING SNIVELING YO-KAI SNOTSOLONG

HEFH
HEFH
WHAT'S WRONG WITH YOU?!
ZLOOSH
ZLOOSH
ZLOOSH
ZLOOSH
WHAAA...
I CAUGHT A COLD AND NOW I HAVE A RUNNY NOSE.
ZLOOOOOSH
YOUR SNOT IS OUT OF CON-TROL!
WHAAAAA?!
I'VE BEEN DRAG-GING IT ALL THIS WAY?!
SNIVELING YO-KAI SNOTSOLONG
NO WONDER I WAS MOVING SO SLOWLY!
BAAM
HOW COULD YOU NOT NOTICE EARLI-ER?!

CAN YOU DO ME A FAVOR?!
LET ME RIDE YOU WHILE YOU FLY! ♪
I'VE ALWAYS WANTED TO SOAR THROUGH THE AIR!
...

AHHH...
?
SPLOO-SH
...CHOOOO!!
MRRRAAAAAOW!!

EWWWW
I'M SORRY...
I'LL FLY YOU AROUND TO MAKE UP FOR IT!

HERE WE GO!
HOORAY! MEOW! ♪
FLAP FLAP

VOOOSH
WHAAAAAT?!
KA-CHUNCK!
THUMP!
NNNNGH!!
I'M SORRY, MY SNOT'S JUST TOO HEAVY...!
HUNH?

EWWWWW
...
OH NO!
I'M SO SORRY!
YOU'RE COVERED IN MY SNOT!
HUUR-GH?!
AGGGGGH...
IT'S COVERING MY MOUTH AND NOSE! I CAN'T BREATHE!
OH NO! HOLD ON! I'LL GET IT OFF RIGHT AWAY!
I JUST NEED TO SUCK IT ALL BACK IN!
SNOOOORT
SNRT SNRT SNRT SNRT
IT'S WORK-ING! IT'S COMING OFF!
HUNH?

I SUCKED IN TOO HARD! HE'S STUCK IN MY NOSE!
THUNGK...
FLAP
FLAP
PLIP
POPT
GAAAAAH!
OWWWWWW!
MNNNGH

?
WHO IS?
FWUP
YOU ARE!
MRRRRAAA OW!
YOU'RE USE-LESS!!
...
TWITCH
TWITCH
TWITCH
JUST GET ON WITH IT AND HELP ME FLY!

AHHHHH...
...
WHAT'S THE MATTER? ARE YOU MAD THAT I CALLED YOU USELESS?

...CHOOOOO!!!
ZLOOOSH
FWAAABT
MEEEEEOW?!
OOPS. SORRY!
FWEEEEEE
AAAAAH...
AT LEAST HE GOT TO FLY!
THUNGKT
MMMNGH...

CHAPTER 10: THE LEGENDARY LUXURIOUS YO-KAI!

FEATURING JEWEL YO-KAI DIANYAN

AHH—HH
I'M NATE ADAMS.
AN ORDINARY ELEMENTARY SCHOOL STUDENT.
WHAT ARE YOU SO HAPPY ABOUT?
I USED MY MONEY FROM THE HOLIDAYS AND BOUGHT...
...A BIKE.
TA—DAAH
WOW! CAN I GIVE IT A TRY?
SURE! BUT HOW WILL YOU RIDE IT WITH NO LEGS?
SHOOMP...
SHOOMP!...

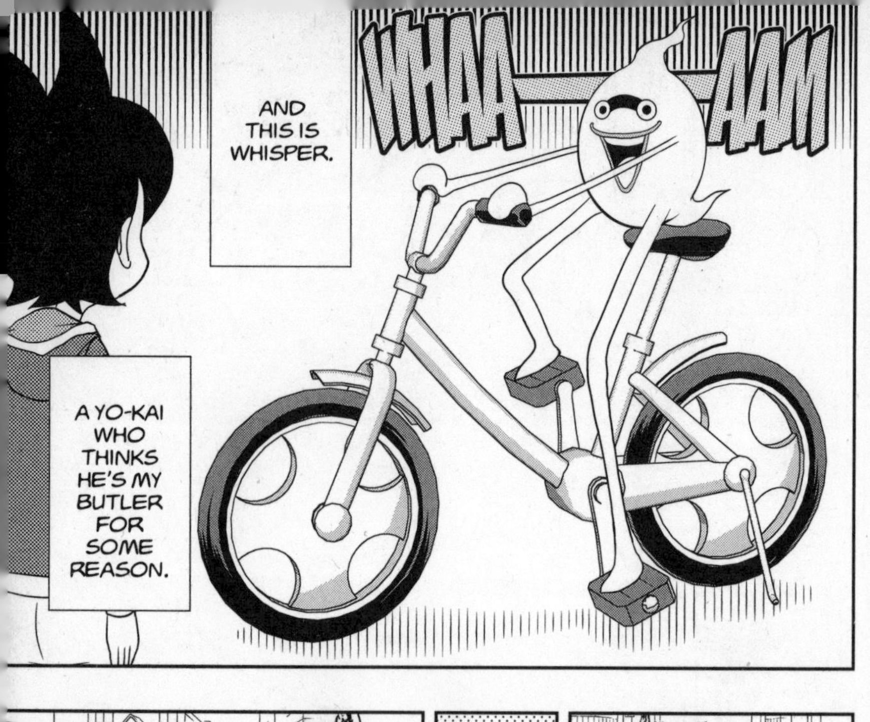
AND THIS IS WHISPER.
WHAA—AAM
A YO-KAI WHO THINKS HE'S MY BUTLER FOR SOME REASON.

!!

HUNH?

SQUEE SQUEE
VNNN...
...

IT'S KATIE! AND SHE'S ON A BIKE TOO! MAYBE WE CAN GO RIDING TOGETHER!

CHARACTER INTRODUCTION
NAME: KATIE FORESTER
NICKNAME: KATIE
THE MOST POPULAR GIRL IN CLASS.

KATIE, LOOK!
I BOUGHT A BIKE TOO...
HUNH?

SIIIIIGH
THE MOST POPULAR GIRL IN CLASS.
HUNH?

SQUEE SQUEE...
WHAT'S THE MAT-TER?

WHY DON'T YOU ASK HER WHAT'S BOTHER-ING HER?

I DON'T KNOW HOW TO TALK TO SOMEONE WHO LOOKS SO DOWN IN THE DUMPS!

THEN WHY DON'T YOU GET HER TALK-ING?
!!!
YOU'RE RIGHT!
RUSTLE
SHLUUUP
CALL-ING...
YO-KAI MEDAL DO YOUR THING!
KRRRKT
FWIPT
VMMMN...

TATTLE-TELL!
TATTLE
TATTLETELL
SHE MAKES PEOPLE SAY WHAT THEY'RE THINKING!
YO-KAI ARE INVISIBLE TO THE HUMAN EYE.
PLIPT
WHAT AM I GOING TO DO? I LOST MY MOM'S DIAMOND RING...
...
I DIDN'T EVEN SEE IT FALL OFF!
DIAMOND RING?!
IT WAS MY MOM'S ABSOLUTE FAVORITE PIECE OF JEWELRY!
KATIE...
I OVERHEARD YOU...
I CAN FIND THE RING FOR YOU!
!!
NATE!
I DON'T KNOW WHY I SAID THAT OUT LOUD...
BUT...

I DON'T THINK YOU'LL BE ABLE TO FIND IT, BUT IT'S A VERY NICE THOUGHT! ♪
...THANKS ANYWAY!
TATTLE
GRIN
?
THAT'S ENOUGH, TATTLE-TELL!
HUMPH
TATTLE! (YOU'RE THE ONE WHO SUMMONED ME!)
WAIT ...

SHE'S NOT EXPECTING MUCH, BUT IF I ACTUALLY FIND IT...
...MAYBE SHE'LL BE SO HAPPY SHE'LL GIVE ME A KISS! ♪
THANK YOU, NATE! ♡
SMACK
NATE! TATTLE-TELL IS HANGING OFF YOUR CHIN!
WHAAAT?! DID KATIE HEAR WHAT I JUST SAID?!
SHE'LL HEAR THIS TOO!

DON'T WORRY! WHILE YOU WERE TALKING SHE WENT BACK TO SEARCHING FOR HER MOM'S RING.
THAT'S SO SAD...
SQUEE
SQUEE
SO...HOW ARE YOU GOING TO DO THIS? DO YOU REALLY THINK YOU CAN FIND THE RING?
EASY. ♪ I'LL GET HELP FROM NOKO!
VOOOOSH
I SEE. ♪
HUNH?
WUBWUBWUB...
ZWOOOSH
WHOA, WHAT IS THAT?!

KRA-
THOOM
ZWOOSH
!!
OWWW I DID IT AGAIN...
WHAT ...?
HE'S A YO-KAI!
HE'S MADE COM-PLETELY OF DIAMOND!
!
STAGGER...
UNNGH...
?!

URRRLLLPT!
SO... DIZZY...
WHAT CAN A DIAMOND PUKE UP?!
URRRGH...
SPLOOOSH!!
HE LOOKS LIKE JIBANYAN! MAYBE THEY'RE RELATED! LIKE SHOGUNYAN?
DO YOU KNOW HIM, WHISPER?
NO...
HEY!
HMM.
KRRRKT
JEWEL YO-KAI
DIANYAN

BUT I THINK THEY JUST REUSED JIBANYAN'S DESIGN...
TATTLE
...BECAUSE HE'S SO POPULAR!!
THIS IS JUST WHISPER'S OPINION!

I SEE.
THANKS, TATTLE-TELL!
TATTLE!
NOOOO...
I CAN'T BELIEVE I SAID THAT OUT LOUD!
THEY REUSED THE DESIGN?!

A DIAMOND YO-KAI SOUNDS PRETTY COOL! ♪
OH! A HUMAN WHO CAN SEE YO-KAI! ♪
I KNOW EXACTLY WHAT YOU'RE THINKING...
?

BAAAM
AS A LOWLY COMMONER, YOU MUST BE IN AWE, TALKING TO A LUXURIOUS DIAMOND YO-KAI LIKE ME!
HE'S LOOKING DOWN ON US!

THAT'S NOT FAIR! I DON'T MEAN TO LOOK DOWN ON YOU.
HUUNH?
DEEP DOWN, I JUST HAPPEN TO KNOW THAT I'M A FAR NOBLER CREATURE THAN YOU ARE! THAT'S ALL!
THAT'S EXACTLY THE PROBLEM!

THAT... THAT MUST BE WHY...I DON'T HAVE ANY FRIENDS!
WAA—AAH
MY INNATE NOBILITY IS THE CAUSE OF ALL OF MY MISFOR-TUNES...
...
I... I...

I WISH I HAD BEEN BORN AS COMMON AND LOWLY AS YOU ARE!
WAAAUGH
SO ANNOYING!
I MAY NOT HAVE ANY FRIENDS...
...BUT BEING SURROUNDED BY MY BEAUTIFUL DIAMONDS BRINGS ME JOY! ♪
KLINK
FWUMPT
ESPECI-ALLY THIS DIAMOND RING I JUST FOUND ON THE STREET! ♪
!!
FOUND ON THE STREET? THAT MUST BE KATIE'S MOM'S RING!
RIGHT!
...
SIGH, YOU KNOW ...

PEOPLE ALWAYS WANT TO CLAIM SOMETHING BELONGS TO THEM ONCE THEY LEARN HOW MUCH IT'S WORTH.
WHAAAAAA
THAT BELONGS TO SOMEONE ELSE! YOU JUST FOUND IT LYING IN THE STREET AND TOOK IT!
YOU'RE A CAT BURG-LAR!

WHAAAAA
A CAT... BURG-LAR?!
TWITCH
TWITCH
ME ...?!

ALL I DID WAS STEAL SOME-THING I FOUND LYING IN THE STREET!
WHAA AA A
FWUMPT
...
HE JUST ADMIT-TED THAT HE STOLE IT!

VERY WELL. IF THAT'S HOW YOU WANT TO PLAY IT...
I GIVE UP.
YES! ♪ KATIE WILL BE SO HAPPY! ♪
FROM NOW ON...

...I WILL EMBRACE MY IDENTITY AS A CAT BURGLAR!
HE'S NOT GOING TO GIVE IT BACK?!
THEN WE'LL TAKE IT FROM YOU BY FORCE!
YO-KAI MED-AL!

KRRRT
DO YOUR THING!

CALLING ...
VNNNNNN

JIBA-NYAN!

HUP.
KA-CHUNGK!
HUNH ?
MEOW! I'M IN THE MIDDLE OF A SHIFT! WHY DID YOU SUMMON ME?!
YOU HAVE A JOB?!
I LOST MY COLLAR ...
...SO I HAVE TO SAVE UP FOR A NEW ONE.
SHUFF SHUFF
HUNH ...?!

HEY! THAT'S MY COLLAR!
I FOUND IT!
!

I FOUND IT LYING ON THE STREET.
A CHEAP GLASS BEAD COLLAR, PAIRED WITH MY BEAUTIFUL DIAMOND BODY...
...IS A VERY FASHION-ABLE MIX!
IT ALL GOES SO WELL TO-GETHER!
IT WAS FATE!
NOT AGAIN ...
THAT'S NOT FUNNY!

I'LL TAKE IT BACK BY FORCE!
CHOOM
CHOOM
CHOOM
CHOOM
CHOOM
TIIIING
YOUR CAT PAW PUNCHES CAN'T HURT MY DIAMOND BODY!
NOT EVEN A SINGLE SCRATCH!

DIIIIIIING
WHAT-EVER. THIS IS WHAT I WAS REALLY AFTER!
OH! THE RING!! THANKS, JIBANYAN!

AIYEEEEEE!
CAT BURGLAR!
LOOK WHO'S TALKING!

I'LL TRADE YOU THE COLLAR! JUST GIVE ME BACK THE RING!

I DON'T WANT THAT PIECE OF JUNK.
THIS IS WAY NICER, SO I'LL KEEP IT INSTEAD. ♪
HE DIDN'T GET IT FOR ME! HE'S GOING TO STEAL IT!
WHAAAA?!

NO!
I DON'T WANT THIS GARBAGE!
KLANK
WUB WUB

HAHAHA! ♪ THAT'S NOT A TOY! ♪
MEOW, MEOW.
WUB WUB
HERE YOU GO!
YEAH!
IT LOOKS SO NICE! ♪
A...
AMY...
!!!

AMY IS THE GIRL WHO JIBANYAN USED TO BELONG TO BEFORE HE BECAME A YO-KAI...
HE SAID HE DIDN'T HAVE ANY MEMORIES FROM BACK THEN, BUT...

I REMEMBER NOW. THAT...
...IS THE COLLAR AMY GAVE TO ME...
?
HOW DARE YOU...
GRRRRN...
HOW DARE YOU THROW AWAY MY BELOVED COLLAR!
YOU JUST CALLED IT A PIECE OF JUNK!
IT'S UNFORGIVABLE!

IF YOU DON'T GIVE ME BACK THE RING, I'LL HAVE TO RESORT TO VIOLENCE!
AND I WARN YOU... MY ENTIRE BODY IS A WEAPON!
!!

WAIT RIGHT THERE! THE ATTACK IS COMING!
TUMP
TUMP
HUFF. HUFF.
TUMP
TUMP
HIS BODY IS SO STIFF HE CAN'T MOVE PROPERLY!
HE'S SO SLOW!
SO WEIRD...
FWUMPT
HE FELL OVER...
IT LOOKS LIKE I'LL HAVE TO USE PLAN B.
?

ZWOOSH
A ROLL ATTACK!
BY SPINNING AROUND, MY TOUGH BODY CAN DESTROY ANYTHING!
SO THAT'S WHY HE WAS ROLLING AROUND EARLIER!
DESTROY ANYTHING?! INTERESTING!
HOW ABOUT THIS?!
KRASH
YAAH!
HEY! THAT'S MY BIKE!

KRUNCH
NOOOOOO!
KRRRR RR RRKKT!

WUB WUB WUB
HELP!
AHHH! STOP FOLLOW-ING US!

SHUPT
?

SO... DIZZY...
URRRLLLPT
AGAIN?!

THIS COLLAR BELONGS TO ME!
WHISPER, CAN YOU TIE IT ON MY NECK? ♪
SURE! ♪
!!

!
LOOK OUT, JIBA-NYAN!

THUNGK!
PERFECT PAWS!

VOOOOOOSH
JIBA-NYAN!

MY DIAMOND PAWS CAN CRUSH MOUNTAINS! NO WAY HE COMES BACK AFTER THAT!

TEMP TEMP
WHOA, THAT WAS INTENSE.
NICE MOVE! ♪
HUNH?!
YOU'RE... OKAY?!
JIBA-NYAN! YOU MADE IT!

YOU USED HIM TO BREAK YOUR FALL?!
NNNGH...
YUP! AND IT WAS ALL THANKS TO WHISPER! ♪
AND ...
I'LL NEVER FORGIVE YOU FOR STEALING THE RING AND DIS-RESPECTING MY COLLAR!
AS LONG AS I KEEP AWAY FROM YOU, I'M NOT SCARED. ♪
KRRKT...
THEN I'LL JUST PUNCH YOU AGAIN! GRRRRAH!
CLOMP
CLOMP...
...
YOUR PUNCHES ARE USELESS AGAINST MY DIAMOND BODY!
VOOOOOSH
TAKE THIS!
PAWS OF...
WAIT... YOU DID THAT!
WHAAAAA
...I'LL GET REVENGE FOR WHAT YOU DID TO WHISPER!!

...
FURY!!
CHOOM
CHOOM
CHOOM
CHOOM
HOOM
OM

CHOOM
CHOOM
YOUR FURRY LITTLE PUNCHES CAN'T HARM ME!
KRRRKT
CHOOM
!!!
CHOOM
!!!
MY BODY... IT'S STARTING TO CRACK...! HOW...?!
CHOOM
YOU'RE FINISHED!
CHOOM
CHOOM

KRA-THOOM!
AAAAAARGH!
WHYYYYYY?!
AN EYE FOR AN EYE, A TOOTH FOR A TOOTH...
A DIAMOND...
...FOR A DIAMOND!
YEAAAH!
YOU PUNCHED HIM WITH KATIE'S DIAMOND RING!
I KNOW! I'LL GLUE HIM BACK TOGETHER!
TINK
TINK
THAT'S NOT HOW YOU HEAL A YO-KAI!
GLUE
...
TUNK
TUNK
BUT DIDN'T YOU GO A LITTLE OVERBOARD?!

TWITCH TWITCH...
ARE YOU... TRYING TO GLUE ME BACK TOGETHER ...?
I'M SORRY! IT'S THE BEST I CAN COME UP WITH!
NO...
GREAT IDEA! KEEP IT UP!
OKAY!
WHAT ?!
GLUE
TA-DAAAH!
HOORAY!
WHAAAA
HE GLUED A YO-KAI?!
!
IN THE PAST, HUMANS WOULD STEAL MY DIAMONDS...
...AND THEN SELL THEM!
SO I FIGURED I MAY AS WELL...
...JUST PICK UP AND KEEP WHATEVER I FOUND...

I DIDN'T KNOW THERE WERE HUMANS AS KIND AS YOU...
I WAS WRONG...
AND I'M SO ASHAMED....

FROM NOW ON, JUST MAKE SURE TO RETURN THINGS TO THE PEOPLE THEY BELONG TO! ♪

YOU GOT IT! ♪

TO SHOW I'M SINCERE, I SHALL BECOME FRIENDS WITH A COMMONER LIKE YOURSELF! ♪
THANKS... I GUESS...
HIS ATTITUDE HASN'T CHANGED AT ALL...

VNNN...

HOORAY! I GOT ANOTHER YO-KAI MEDAL! ♪
POOPT

USE THIS TO BUY YOURSELF ANOTHER BICYCLE. ♪
WHAT? YOU'RE GIVING ME A DIA-MOND?!

SURE! FEEL FREE TO USE MY LEFT LEG! ♪
WHAAAA
NO... THAT'S OKAY... YOU CAN HAVE IT BACK!

I JUST WANTED TO GET KATIE'S RING BACK.
DON'T YOU WANT ANY-THING FOR YOUR-SELF?

OF COURSE I DO! ♡
THANK YOU, NATE!

OKAY, JIBANYAN. THE RING...

VOOO—SH
HEY! HE'S GETTING AWAY WITH THE RING!
WHAT?! STOP!

NATE! WHERE ARE YOU?
OH...
VOOOOSH
SPLUNGK!
AAAARGH!
YO-KAI ARE INVISIBLE TO THE HUMAN EYE.
LATER, NATE!
HOO-RAY! ♪
I HAVE TO RETURN IT BEFORE MY MOM KNOWS IT'S MISSING! ♪
WHAAAAA?
VOOOOSH
OH!
THE RING!
TINK...
TWITCH TWITCH...
DID I RUN OVER SOME-THING ...?
TOO BAD, YOU TWO...
SQUEE SQUEE...
TWITCH TWITCH...
NATE ADAMS' CURRENT NUMBER OF YO-KAI FRIENDS: 21

NATE VERSUS JIBANYAN?!

FROM THE NINTENDO 3DS GAME, YO-KAI WATCH.

DID YOU FIND ALL FIVE OF THE BONUS FUNNIES? IF YOU'VE ONLY FOUND FOUR, TRY LOOKING FOR THE FIFTH ONE! ♪

SPECIAL CHAPTER: YO-KAI INTRODUCTIONS!

...
EVERY-
ONE'S
FAVOR-
ITE...
...
YOU
HAVE
...
TU MP
...AS
LONG
AS...
SH UFF
HEY!
GET THE
SPOTLIGHT
ON ME!
TA—DA!
...JIBA-
NYAN!
OK!
EVERY-
ONE
READY?
♪
LET'S
GO!
♪

JIBANYAN

MEOW, MEOW! ♪

BOING BOING

GOLDENYAN

I JUST BECAME FRIENDS WITH A GOLDEN ROBONYAN!
THIS YO-KAI WILL BE SUPER USEFUL! ♪
THIIII——NG
YES, HE'S VERY POW-ERFUL! ♪

I NEED YOU TO COME WITH ME!
?
AN EVERY-MART ?!
ZWOOOSH
OVER HERE.
Everymart

WE'LL BUY IT FOR $10,000!
GREAT!
WHAAAAA?!
THAT'S ALL THAT HE WANTED TO DO WITH HIM?!
HE SOLD HIM?!

YOU CAN SELL THINGS YOU DON'T NEED AT EVERYMART.

BLAZION
REALLY INTENSE GUYS GET ON MY NERVES...
GRRAH!!
BLAZE BLAZE BLAAAZE! (A BOY LIKE YOU SHOULD BE WORKING TO ACHIEVE HIS DREAMS!)
HE CAN ONLY SPEAK USING THE WORD "BLAZE."
BLAZE! (DO YOU FEEL IT?! DO YOU FEEL YOUR HEART BLAZING?!)
NNGH
FWOOSH
BLAAAZE! (INJECTING A BLAZING HEART!)
AAAAGH!
GEEZ! QUIET DOWN!
BLAZE, BLAZE BLAZE! (CHILDREN SHOULD BE LIVELY! AND CHEERFUL!)
GRRRR RAAAAAH!
BLAAAAZE! (NOW HE'S JUST BLAZING AND ANNOYED!)
AAAAAARGH! YOU'RE SO ANNOYING!
BEAT IT, YOU FLAMING FURBALL!
WHAAAA?!

REUKNIGHT

I'M COUNTING ON YOU, MOCHISMO!
I AM YOUR HONORABLE OPPONENT.

THUNGKT
YEAH!

HIS HEAD FELL OFF?!
HEH HEH HEH...
WUB WUB WUB
HE'S BROKEN INTO HIS TWO ORIGINAL PIECES:
HELMSMAN AND ARMSMAN!
BUT THAT MEANS...

MOCHISMO! BEHIND YOU!
!!!

FWIISH
FWIISH
WOOSH
...
HE CAN'T SEE WITHOUT HIS HEAD...
FWOOSH
HUNH?!

SNEE
FWOOOOO...
RRRRRooo
WHAT A SPOOKY YO-KAI...
BLOOD... I NEED BLOOD...

!
BRING IT ON!
I'LL STOP YOU!
SHUFF
WE HAVE TO DO SOME-THING! THIS YO-KAI IS DANGER-OUS!
THAT EVIL SWORD MUST MAKE HIM CRAVE BLOOD!
FWOOOOO

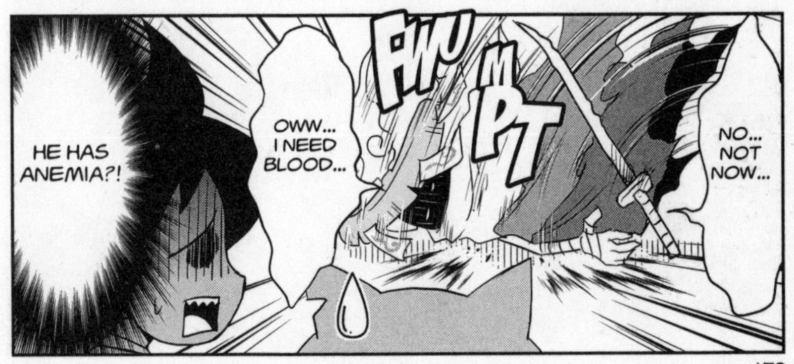
HE HAS ANEMIA?!
OWW... I NEED BLOOD...
FWUMPT
NO... NOT NOW...

CUPISTOL

YOU CAN MAKE A GIRL FALL IN LOVE WITH ME?! THAT'S AMAZING!
WHICH GIRL?
WAAH
WAAH
WAAH
WAAH

THE ONE IN THE MID-DLE!
TEE-HEE
TEE-HEE
WAAH WAAH
OKAY!

VOOOOOSH
DON'T WORRY! I NEVER MISS!

CHOOM
VOOOOSH
UH OH...

NATE...
AHH...
NOOOOO...
WHOOPS!

MAD MOUNTAIN

CHOOMCHOOMCHOOM
SUMO PAWS OF FURY!
WHEN YOU'VE BEEN PUSHED TO THE EDGE... THAT'S WHEN SUMO GETS INTER-ESTING!
SHUMP

YAAAAAAH!
FWAAAAAP
MRRAAAAOW!
JIBANYAN!

WHEN I'M AT THE EDGE OF THE SUMO RING, NO ONE CAN...
VNNN...

...DE-FEAT ME--
VROOM
THUNGKT
GRAAH!

TENGU

FOOOOOSH
WHAAAA-AAAT?!
TAKE THAT!

FSSSH...
FWOOM

FWIP FWIP
AS LONG AS I HOLD IT... I'M INVINCIBLE!

THUNCK
I CAN BLOW ANYONE AWAY JUST BY SWINGING MY FAN! ♪

...
...
HE SWUNG THE FAN AT HIMSELF!
FOOOOOSH
AAAAAAAAH!

PUPSICLE

JUST LOOKING AT YOU IS MAKING ME FEEL COLD!
I'M... F-F-F-FREEZ-ING!
TRREMBBLE TRREMBBLE
SHUDDER SHUDDER
SHUDDER SHUDDER
TRREMBBLE TRREMBBLE

BLAZION!
BLAAAAAZE!
FSSSSH
HOW DO YOU FEEL NOW?

WHSSSSH
HE'S MELT-ING!
DRIP
DRIP
DRRRIP...

KOMASAN

I CAN'T WAIT TO FIND A NEW PLACE TO REST MY HEAD!
TEMP TEMP
MEOW. MEOW.
HUH?
MEOW MEOW
YOU AIN'T GOT NO HOME EITHER, DO YA? POOR LITTLE VARMINT...
PLEASE LOOK AFTER ME!
BUT EVERYBODY'S GOTTA STRIKE OUT ON THEIR OWN.
GIT ALONG NOW! YER FREE!
MEOW. ♪

DON'T YOU WORRY NONE, I GOT THIS. ♪
WHAA—AA?!
SNIFF. SNIFF.
PLEASE LOOK AFTER ME!
HUNH?!
MRRRR-AAAOW! (YOU TOOK MY BOX! THAT'S NOT FAIR!)

WIGLIN
WOOOHOOO!
I'M WIGLIN AND I LOVE SEAWEED! ♪
WIGGLE
WIGGLE
YEAH!
WHAT KIND OF WEIRD YO-KAI IS THAT?!

OUT OF MY WAY!
PAWS OF FURY!
CHOOM CHOOM CHOOM
FSSH FSSH FSSH
YOU CAN'T HIT ME! ♪ I AVOID YOUR PUNCHES AS EASILY AS SWAYING IN THE SEA! ♪
GRRRN
I CAN DODGE ANY ATTACK! NO ONE CAN DEFEAT ME!
VRRRROOOOOM...
GRR RAA AAH!
...
THUNGKT

AUNTIE HEART
COME TO AUNTIE! ♪
HUG...
WHAT IS SHE DOING?
OH! THAT'S AUNTIE HEART...

I'LL BE A GOOD YO-KAI FROM NOW ON! ♪
AWWW...
...SHE CAN MAKE ANY YO-KAI GOOD AND PURE JUST BY HUGGING THEM.
HMM.
JIBANYAN, YOU'VE BEEN PRETTY SELFISH LATELY. WHY DON'T YOU LET HER HUG YOU?
WHAT? A HUG ISN'T ENOUGH TO CHANGE ME!
COME HERE

THUMP T...
IF YOU DON'T TURN OVER A NEW LEAF, I'LL SNAP YOUR SPINE IN TWO!
PSST PSST
KRRKT KRRKT
KRRKT...
I... WILL... I PROM-ISE!
SHE'S JUST THREAT-ENING THEM TO MAKE THEM BEHAVE!

EVERFORE

WILL YOU BE MY FRIEND?
HEE HEE
SURE, OF COURSE! ♪
HOORAY!
SHE'S SO CUTE! ♡

WHAT DO YOU DO FOR FUN?
HEE HEE HEE
IT'S SO EMBARRASSING... I LIKE TO EAT! ♪
LET'S GO GET SOMETHING TOGETHER THEN! ♪

ARE YOU OK? YOU'RE NOT EATING MUCH...
CHOMP CHOMP
OH, DON'T WORRY... I AM. ♪

OKEE DOKE! ♪
CHOMP CHOMP
SLOOOSH
LUNCH $7.00
DINNER $8.80
I'M EATING YOUR LIFE! ♡
HA HA HA HA!

ROLLEN

A YO-KAI WHO DECIDES EVERYTHING BY ROLLING HIS DICE EYES, HUH?
WUB
WUB
I'LL ROLL MY DICE EYES TO DECIDE IF YOU'RE MY ENEMY!

YOU'RE SURE TAKING YOUR TIME...
WUB
WUB
WUB

WUB WUB
HMM... LET'S SEE...!
I HOPE IT'S ANOTHER GOOD ONE!

LUCKY ROLL! WE'RE NOT ENEMIES!
TUNK
SO, YOU'LL BE MY FRIEND?

WUB WUB
WUB WUB

WUB WUB WUB
OWWW...
HE MADE HIMSELF DIZZY!
WHAT?!

MANJIMUTT
WHY AM I CURSED WITH THIS FACE...?
IF ONLY I HAD A FACE...

...LIKE THIS!
...OR LIKE THIS! NO ONE WOULD BE SCARED OF ME THEN!
NO...

YOUR FACE ISN'T THE PROBLEM!
WHA——AAA?
?

DO YOU REALLY THINK THAT FUNNY FACES ARE ENOUGH TO MAKE PEOPLE LAUGH THESE DAYS?
...
WENT INTO THE BATH-ROOM AND SAW--
WHAP
...
THE SAME GOES FOR DIRTY JOKES!
YOUR SENSE OF HUMOR IS TOO CORNY!

I WANTED TO BE THE CREAM OF THE CROP*... BUT YOU THINK I'M CORNY!
WHA AAA
HE MADE ANOTHER JOKE OUT OF IT! AT LEAST HE'S TRYING...

*THE CREAM OF THE CROP: THE ABSOLUTE BEST!

DRAGGIE

I'LL USE THE CRYSTAL BALL ON MY HEAD TO FIND OUT WHAT POWERS YOU HAVE!

WHAAAA
IT'S ME! I'M IN THE CRYSTAL BALL!
VWOO
VWOO

AHHHH
WHAT'S IT SAY? WHAT'S IT SAY?! I CAN'T SEE!
SHUFF SHUFF
I CAN'T REACH IT! SOMEONE HELP ME GET IT DOWN!
VOOOSH
WHY ARE SO MANY YO-KAI SO STUPID?
SORRY... MEOW.

DAIZ
DAAAAAZE
YOU'RE ALWAYS SO SPACED OUT.

BLAZION!
BLAAA-AZE!
FWOOOSH

FWOOOOOOSH
DAAAAAZE
NOW HE'S BLAZING AND SPACED OUT!

VENOCT

YOUR DRAGON SCARVES ARE REALLY COOL! ♪

GO!
OF COURSE! THEY'RE MY FRIENDS, AND THEY OBEY MY EVERY COM-MAND!

AS LONG AS THEY'RE WITH ME, I CAN KEEP FIGHTING EVEN IF I'M SURROUNDED!
WHAT? THE SCARVES ARE ALIVE?

SHUNGKT...
ULLLLPT!
NO...! GO IN... THE SAME... DIRECTION!
WHAAAA ?!
VOOSH
VOOSH

SHOGUNYAN

I HEAR THAT YOU'RE TAKING GOOD CARE OF MY DESCENDANT. ♪
TO SHOW MY GRATI- TUDE...
SHUFF SHUFF
HOORAY! HE'S GOING TO PAY ME! ♪

BAAM
PLEASE ACCEPT THIS.
A BONITO FISH ?!

WHOOPS! HUMANS PREFER THIS, DON'T THEY?
SHUFF SHUFF
THIS IS BETTER... ♪

HERE!
A TUNA...

(YO-KAI WATCH VOLUME 3 END / CONTINUED IN VOLUME 4)

TA- DAAH
THE YO-KAI MEDAL !!
A MEDAL GIVEN TO YOU BY THE YO-KAI YOU BEFRIEND.

VNNN NN NN NN NN
CALLING ...
YOU CAN SUMMON THAT YO-KAI ANYTIME YOU WANT.
NNN
NN NN NN

JIBA-NYAN!!

CRRSH
VRRRM—
BUT BE CAREFUL WHERE YOU SUMMON THEM.
OOPS, SORRY.

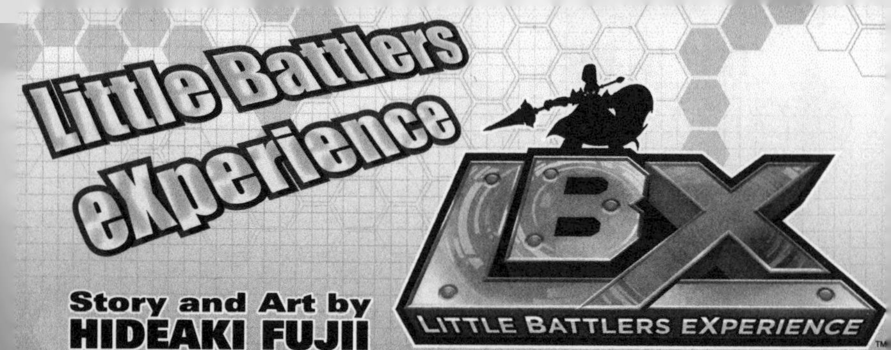
Little Battlers eXperience
LBX
LITTLE BATTLERS EXPERIENCE™
Story and Art by
HIDEAKI FUJII

LBX
LITTLE BATTLERS EXPERIENCE
1
2
3
4
5
6
Story and Art by
HIDEAKI FUJII

THIS IS THE END OF THIS GRAPHIC NOVEL!

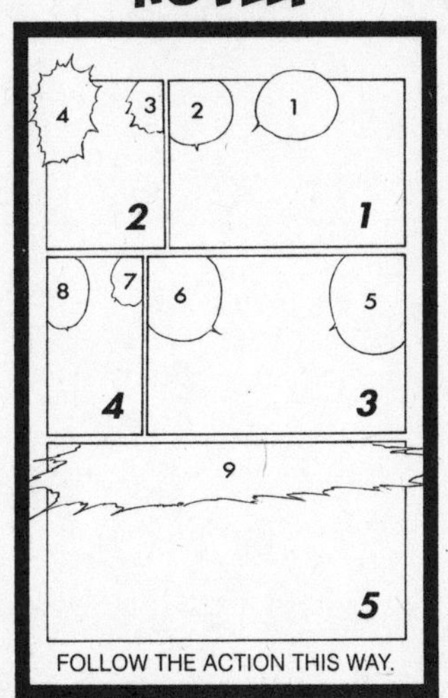
FOLLOW THE ACTION THIS WAY.

To properly enjoy this Perfect Square graphic novel, please turn it around and begin reading from right to left.

YO-KAI WATCH

KCH KCH
WHAT? THE LIGHT WON'T COME OUT.

MAYBE IT'S OUT OF BATTER-IES?
DO YOU REALLY THINK THE YO-KAI WATCH WORKS ON A BATTERY?

I SEE...
RRRMBB
IT MUST MOVE ON A MUCH MORE AMAZING POWER SOURCE.

GRRRCH GRRRCH
HERE!!
IT'S A WIND-UP WATCH ?!

AUTHOR BIO

I'm enjoying "make believe Yo-kai Watch" with my four-year-old daughter.
—Noriyuki Konishi

Noriyuki Konishi hails from Shimabara City in Nagasaki Prefecture, Japan. He debuted with the one-shot *E-CUFF* in *Monthly Shonen Jump Original* in 1997. He is known for writing manga adaptations of *AM Driver* and *Mushiking: King of the Beetles*, along with *Saiyuki Hiro Go-Kū Den!*, *Chōhenshin Gag Gaiden!! Card Warrior Kamen Riders*, *Go-Go-Go Saiyuki: Shin Gokūden* and more.